WAVING BACKWARDS

A Savannah Novel

V.L. Brunskill

Published by:
Southern Yellow Pine (SYP) Publishing
4351 Natural Bridge Rd.
Tallahassee, FL 32305

www.syppublishing.com

This is a work of fiction. Names, characters, places, and events that occur either are the products of the author's imagination or are used fictitiously with the exception of Felix de Weldon. The sculptor's actions in this work are also fictitious. Any resemblance to actual persons, places, or events is purely coincidental.

ISBN-10: 1-940869-36-6
ISBN-13: 978-1-940869-36-0
ISBN-13: ePub 978-1-940869-39-1
Library of Congress Control Number: 2015940315

Printed in the United States of America
First Edition
May 2015

Praise for the Author

In her debut novel, music journalist to the stars, V.L Brunskill, intricately weaves the very complex issues of a modern day Northern adoption-seeker into the historical quilt and Southern charm of a place I now call home. Brava! *Waving Backwards: A Savannah Novel,* has something for every reader.

Bertice Berry, PhD.,
Best-Selling Author of Redemption Song and
The Ties That Bind

Waving Backwards is a compelling reminder of the need we all feel to know who we are and where we came from, and when that quest comes with a cryptic clue, a memorable romance and the charm only a city like Savannah can provide, we rush along with determined Lara Bonavito to uncover the ultimate truths.

John Warley,
Author of *A Southern Girl*, *Bethesda's Child*,
and *The Moralist*.

ii

Dedication

For both of my mothers
(who gave all),

For my husband
(who never wants to hear about Robert again),

For my precious daughter Nia
(who charges me a quarter every time I mention my book),

And for the people of Savannah
(who have allowed this Yankee to call their city home).

Acknowledgments

Grateful acknowledgments to the following:

First reader and friend Gloria Shearin
Richmond Hill Public Library Book Club
A.K. Clarke Editing
Georgia Historical Society
Savannah Marriott Riverfront
Savannah's Candy Kitchen
Savannah Area Chamber of Commerce
NYC Domestic Abuse Hotline operated by Safe Horizon

Imagine not knowing who you are, until
you find yourself
in a statue
800 miles from home.

Chapter 1

March 16, 1991

Not for the first time, the third floor apartment at 6839 Cloverdale Boulevard in Babylon, New York, suffers an early morning onslaught of spillage and slamming.

"I don't care what the damned letter says!" Maureen roars, pounding the FTD smiley-face mug on the countertop, sending a great wave of coffee across the linoleum floor. "You're not going anywhere."

Finally freed from three feverish days of battling the flu, Lara stands in a patch of morning sun too bright for the argument. Bringing up the letter and explaining that she has opted out of the summer internship at *Long Island News* unleashes her mother's well-oiled temper. Maureen tugs at the belt of her terrycloth robe. She has worn the once lavish birthday gift—from the monster—for a decade, despite its wash-bled salmon color.

"Look, Ma," says Lara, wiggling her toes and staring at the chipped, red polish she meant to repaint the week before. It is the same crimson shade as her mother's face. "I'm going wherever the letter takes me. There's a student loan check coming at the end of May and another in the fall. I'll skip a semester if I have to, but this is my life."

"Your life. What about my life?" Maureen asks through gritted teeth. "I'm working my ass off to pay for school, and you're already behind. Who starts college at nineteen anyway?

You've pissed away a whole year, and you're not taking that money and heading off to…God knows where."

Outrage outranks guilt, and Lara says, too harshly, "I need to know where I come from. Don't I deserve to know who I look like? Who I act like? My medical information?"

"You act like me. You look like your grandfather. They matched us up perfectly," Maureen mutters, pressing both palms hard against her forehead to relieve the tension of the lie.

"Uh, how do I resemble Grandpa?" Lara's neediness turns to indignation. "He's black Italian and I'm as white as a ghost. Get real." Leaving the sunny halo, Lara leans against the fridge for support. Her shoulder dislodges a photo of her pre-med cousin from under a banana-shaped magnet. Lara looks nothing like the rest of her family. The waifish girl in the photo has brooding dark eyes and a thick mane of black hair. Adoption makes Lara particularly uncommon. In her opinion, she does not look like a Bonavito, an Italian, or a New Yorker.

"Get real?" Maureen booms, her pointer finger upsettingly close to Lara's face. "I'll tell you what's real: paying the bills so you can get a degree and not work crap jobs anymore. I left your father to make things better, not for you to trash your life, chasing a fantasy."

"You married the idiot and let him beat us for years…so why should I…?" Lara inhales deeply, as if trying to suck the words back in. Unsuccessful, she tenses for the slap she knows her mother will deliver. Maureen moves within striking distance. As usual, the sting is less painful on Lara's face than in her heart. With a flip of her hair and well-placed sleeve, Lara wipes away the tears before Maureen can see them.

Maureen paces, a captive lioness, crossing back and forth in front of the half-removed orange and yellow fruit wallpaper, one of many renovations abandoned for lack of money and motivation. "Okay, Lara, I'm sorry. I am sorry, I just…you made your point. If you want to take the money and blow it, okay, but I'm not paying any more tuition. You hear me?"

Maureen bends to wipe up the spilled coffee, exposing her nakedness beneath the robe.

Lara looks away, hoping to preserve at least that much of her mother's dignity. "Fine, Mom, whatever you want." There is no need to say anything more. Maureen has acquiesced, and that is all Lara needs to move forward.

Lara retreats to her room, stopping to study the framed images of her olive-skinned relatives who line the hallway. Their gregarious, open expressions confuse and calm her. They are the only family she has ever known. Still, the missing images of blood relatives haunt her. Lara turns the bent hanger shoved into the hollow where the doorknob had broken off and enters her room. Self-doubt follows, and Lara struggles to decide which evil she will choose. "Do I hurt her or keep living the lie?" She asks the dated pop-star posters that dangle from taped and tacked pedestals.

"Why can't she understand the danger of being blank?" Lara continues, talking to the magnificent males that were once a haven of teenage titillation and hope. "Well, Mr. Gibb," she says, "do you think I should tell her that I slept with ten guys last year, just to feel a bond with someone?"

For a boozy year after high school graduation, Lara waited tables at Grover's Pub. A thigh-high uniform and party atmosphere provided a steady stream of men and the sort of made-up connections that fertilize loneliness. Beaches, park benches and vans were the sordid scenes of her desperation. Closing her eyes, she can imagine every crease and crinkle of the bronzed poster boys on her walls but cannot visualize a single feature of the men she slept with.

Lara checks her face in the mirror to be sure the angry handprint has faded before heading down the hall to find her mother. Maureen stares at the console television, still not dressed for her noon shift at the dry cleaners. When she hears Lara approaching, Maureen pretends to be engrossed in a game show.

5

Sitting next to Maureen, Lara finds her peacemaking voice. "Mom, I'll finish college." Her mother's eyes stray to the Bible, still open to the page where Lara discovered the envelope. Lara closes it and puts it back under the table, hoping this gesture will end the battle.

"I get a student loan check at the end of next semester. I'll skip summer classes so the September grant will cover fall tuition. I will only use one check, I promise."

Covering Maureen's calloused hand with her own, Lara tries to comfort her, "It's okay, Mom. It's going to be okay."

Maureen says nothing.

Chapter 2

March 15, 1991

L ara would have languished in the heated stupor of the flu longer, if not for the letter. The day before she informed Maureen that she intended to find her family, Lara lay on the plaid couch, wrung out from retching.

Examining her ashen reflection in the glass of the coffee table, she had grimaced at the tangled nest of over-highlighted blonde hair that hung across her tea-green eyes. Ashamed of the fifteen freshman pizza pounds that jellied her mid-section, she was stretching out the stomach area of her Led Zeppelin T-shirt when she noticed the sliver of white at the center of the ornate family Bible.

Always more curious than cautious, Lara slid the envelope from its decades-old hiding place. The note-sized sheet of paper wore a rubbery residue, as if torn from a pad. Lara picked at the glue as she read the shaky script for the first time.

The baby's roots are with the Southern lady
who waves forever.
Her heart was Pearced and so was that of
her mother.
Pearced was she by the cotton race that will
never end.
Buried in the first city is a man who holds
the 9th key.

The page lacked a date or signature. Lara sat scissor straight on the couch as the significance of the letter took shape in the fuzzy fluid of her fevered brain. More alert than she'd been in days, Lara juggled the circus of words, needing to unravel the letter's meaning.

Lara is an only child. This made it easy to decide that she was the baby mentioned in the letter. The rest of the message was far less clear. The "waving one" could mean a flag. "Southern" could mean the Southern USA or the South Coast of Long Island. A fastidious speller, Lara's focus narrowed to the word "Pearce." Misspelled twice with a capital P, Lara thought. Pierced is the proper spelling for stabbed. A name?

Lara tasted salty perspiration as she covered the cavernous shock of her agape mouth. Fireworks exploded in her head as she realized what she had found.

"Holy Moses," she screeched. "Is it my name...my real name?"

After finding the letter, Lara called her mother at work. A hideously altered and depressing cover version of an Elton John song played in the background as she waited on hold. Her mother picked up just in time to save Lara from a droning mutilation of the chorus.

"Lara, we're so busy. Feeling better?" Maureen asked in a sweet, singsong sales voice.

"Mom, I found a letter in the Bible," Lara said cautiously. "Sounds like it's about my birth family. Where did you get it?" Her feet planted on the gray throw rug in front of the couch, Lara listened with rapt attention.

"What? Hang on a sec," Maureen said over shuffling papers and the muffled voice of a customer. Lara waited, eager and nauseous from a mix of finally found familial possibilities and the emotional undoing the conversation would have on her mother.

"When did you put it in the Bible?" asked Lara impatiently.

8

"Well, I…the Bible? Oh," said Maureen, pausing, as if searching for the right words. "I, uh…I meant to mention it, but it doesn't say anything. I didn't want to get your hopes up."

"My hopes?" Lara asked angrily, her fists clenching. "For Christ's sake, Mom. I've asked you a million times, and you had the letter all along?" Lara stood and the patchwork quilt slipped to her feet. She stretched out a shaking hand to reveal the wrinkled result of her anger on the precious, identity-giving page.

"Can we talk about this when I get home?" asked Maureen, clearing her throat nervously.

"Just tell me where you got it," Lara seethed, biting the inside of her cheek to stop from slinging angry accusations.

Sweat slithered from Lara's bra to her belly button as the heat of the fever and her predicament built to a firestorm. Lara removed an ice-cube from the overturned cup at her feet, running it across her face as she tried to listen, learn, and cool down.

"It was behind your hospital photo." Maureen's voice was shrill and whiny; a child caught stealing a coveted toy. "I didn't find it 'til you were one or two. It was in the photo card. I'm sorry, Lara. It's nothing. Let's talk when I get home. Okay?"

Lara searched for a non-venomous word to utter and waited until silence spurned a soft click, indicating that her mother had cut the connection. Lara could not believe her mother had called the letter "nothing." She gripped the handset to her chest. Outrage seasoned with guilt clung to the air of the family room, adding a static heaviness to the viral congestion in her pounding head. Lara considered the weight of the question along with her right to ask it; questioning the mother who raised her felt disrespectful. No matter how much they suffered, at least this mother had stayed.

Her mother's dismissive tone chimed in again, "It's nothing, Lara."

If it is nothing, Lara surmised, *then so am I.*

Protect her! The voice in her head made Lara flinch.

Why should I? She did not protect me from him. Lara wrestled a guilty need to please the woman who saved her from the smoldering ruins of foster care, only to place her in the fiery hands of her adoptive father.

Chapter 3

Two days after Maureen's defeated agreement that Lara could use school money to pursue the clues of the letter, Lara grins greedily at the collection of suddenly useful encyclopedias spread on the plywood floor of the walk-in closet. With several volumes opened, Lara references a map of the United States, locating a few prominent cotton plantations mentioned in Volume 4. Like a surfer eyeing the promise of every wave, Lara reviews the clues of the letter, flipping through a universe of words to find the ones that belong to her.

In the P pages, she looks for Pearces. The surname reveals only a few British authors and an English boxer. No mention of anyone related to cotton, waving, or the south. So far, nothing paves her path. Maureen has given Lara permission to pursue the clues, but she has no idea where to begin.

Lara rereads the mysterious jumble of words, "Who is the Southern lady who waves forever?"

Lara figures that since she was born in New York, she should stick to the East Coast. She yanks the heavy leather book to her lap, examining the U.S. map again. Making a list of the Southern states on the yellow-lined pad that was blank until now, she writes; Florida, Georgia, Maryland, North Carolina, South Carolina, Virginia, West Virginia, and the District of Columbia. Lara numbers the list. There are eight possibilities. It could be worse.

Lara focuses her attention now on finding the "first cities" of each state. A confusing city unto itself, she draws a line though the District of Columbia. Now down to seven states, Lara's arms ache as she lifts each heavy volume. She finds the information she needs, adding the first cities for each state to her list.

- Florida: St. Augustine
- South Carolina: Charleston
- Virginia: Jamestown
- Georgia: Savannah
- Maryland: St. Mary's
- North Carolina: Bath
- West Virginia: Wheeling

Volume 16, with entries for SA–SE, rests on Lara's right knee, prompting her to look for Savannah. Turning bunches of pages at a time, she finds that Savannah garners a half-page in the periodical. There are color photographs of arching trees and descriptions of places called River Street and Forsyth Park. The page describes Savannah as "an industrial seaport on the Savannah River."

Lara examines a historic photo of a mansion with a two-sided staircase and an ornate ironwork gate. The fancy façade reminds Lara of Vincenzo's Palazzo, the Long Island wedding venue where her aunt was married. Lara had felt conspicuous and ridiculous amid the reception room's crystal baubles and nude, plaster sculptures. Everything about Vincenzo's was overdone. Even the entranceway intimidated with its Hollywood style searchlights that swept the building and sky at two-minute intervals. In the photo, gas lanterns flank the Southern mansion's entranceway. The image makes it look as if the modern world skipped Savannah. Lara sighs at the other-worldliness and serenity of the picture.

Lara reads on, "Georgia's state flower is the Cherokee Rose." She has never seen such a thorny flower in her life.

"Oh my...," Lara's cheek quivers. At the bottom of page is a woman waving what looks like a towel. Under it, the caption reads, "Savannah's Waving Girl: Florence Martus."

"Are you my mother?" asks Lara, giddy from the find and the memory of a favorite childhood storybook. In that book, a delightfully confused cartoon bird utters Lara's secret question to everything it encounters, even inanimate objects. "Are you my mother? Are you my mother? Are you my mother?" Lara laughs at the memory.

The tiny photo and caption are the only mention of the Waving Girl. Savannah is the first city of Georgia and they have a waving chick. The idea of spending her loan money on a trip to the Southern jewel fascinates her. Leaving out all of the other Southern states and assuming that the letter refers to the East Coast is sloppy, but it could still be right.

Lara clears the floor, haphazardly re-shelving the books to avoid piquing another motherly inquisition. With a final push, she wedges the stubborn last volume onto the sloped shelf before grabbing her keys. Next stop is the Be Happy Travel Agency.

Busybody Bea Bailey stops her at the door. Lara recognizes a hornet's nest of questions buzzing in Bea's eyes.

"Hi, Bea. I'm looking for anything you have on Savannah."

"Reaaaalllllllly? When're you heading to the Southern jewel? Do tell me more, Lara," Bea wheezes with high-pitched excitement. "Does your mother know you're going? Where will you stay?"

Lara grins at her, deciding how to respond.

"Are you going for business? Pleasure? Bringing a few friends from school, I suppose. Nothing like a trip with the girls.

When I was at NYU, we had the loveliest time in London, and—"

"Not sure, Bea," Lara replies hurriedly. "Can I have whatever brochures you have?"

"So, Lara, how is school anyway?" Bea salivates. "Any luck on the relationship front?"

"Not yet," says Lara. She shuffles her feet impatiently. "About those brochures?"

Like a woodpecker attacking a single spot of exposed bark until barren, Bea continues, "Is your mother still working all those jobs? I don't have a clue how she manages. Just thinking about that dry-cleaning place makes my hair frizz."

Obviously exhausted by the prospect of doing anything more physical than handing over a travel brochure, Bea pats her hair down and warns, "It'll be hot in Savannah this time of year. Are you ready for that heat? If you wait until October, it'll be much more tolerable. Maybe you and your mother are related after all. Both of you can handle the heat…if ya know what I mean."

Lara half-smiles, considering how to react to the off-handed comment about her adopted status. Bea lacks a filter, but Lara understands the source of her endless prattle. Lara attended high school with Bea's daughter, Ashley. A popular, pride-inducing teen, Ashley was everything Lara wished to be. While Lara hung out with fellow wallflowers at the senior prom, Ashley twirled across the dance floor all night with Chip Darrent, captain of the football team.

After the wreck, the local news reported that Ashley and Chip had planned to marry. Chip's MG Midget folded like a taco under the semi, killing the teens instantly. No one knew about the baby until afterwards, and the sorrow of losing an unborn grandchild and child broke something in Bea, who started talking at the funeral and never stopped.

Lara fiddles with the faux pearl finish of her shirt buttons as Bea continues to purge. Lara's lack of response stirs Bea to action. "Well, let me see what I've got."

Bea hands over a tri-fold Savannah brochure with a photo of a swim-sized swan fountain on the front.

"Thanks." Lara grabs the brochure, and starts a slow, backward retreat from Bea's inquiries. She stops when she spots the desperation under Bea's over-glued, false eyelashes.

"Bea, could you help me get a decent hotel discount?" Lara asks faintly. She opens the brochure. There, in living color, is the waving chick. "I'd like to be close to this statue." Lara points at the photograph, tilting it so that Bea can see.

"Oh my, well of course I can, Lara," Bea's voice yo-yos excitedly. "Please sit, child. I'll find you something safe. Don't want your mother crazed about you girls." Bea's hands fly across the keyboard and the questions continue. "How many of you are there? Will you need me to book a flight?"

"I'm going alone and I'm driving," states Lara in a clear voice.

Bea's voice shifts into fifth gear. "Alone! Are you sure? I mean, Savannah is lovely, but couldn't you take someone? You can't be too careful. Driving, well, I don't think...does your mother know about this?"

"Yes." Lara stares at Bea, attempting to convey that she will not be divulging anything more. "I'd like to leave after finals, first week of June, please."

Bea looks up from her screen to Lara's determined expression. "Well, I'll pull some strings, Lara. I can't put you anywhere dangerous, especially alone. In fact, I'll use my agent discount. It's the least I can do for a classmate of—" Bea stops before saying her daughter's name, the only word that has not graced her lips since the accident.

Lara walk-skips away from the agency, relieved to escape poor Bea's chirping, and ecstatic that trip planning is underway.

The baby's roots are with the Southern
lady who waves forever.

Chapter 4

June 2, 1991

Whirring past cars in a haze of haphazard thinking and driving, Lara reflects on the letter, pulling it repeatedly from the passenger seat to review the words as questions squawk in her head. What if her family owned slaves? Will she find a bunch of bigoted old folks who look down their noses at her? Will they like her? Will there be brothers or sisters? How will she find them?

Her mind lingers on the last question as several states whir by. Before the letter, everything she knew about her origin came from Child's Aid. They handled the adoption and penned an intentionally vague one-page report that included only the time and date of her birth and her adoptive parent's names.

Questions and possibilities make it impossible to focus. Other drivers fly past, waving aggravated hands as she swerves to grab the letter. Billboards advertising cheap hotel rooms, free breakfasts, and bottomless cups of coffee call to her, yet she pushes on, hoping to make the drive from New York to Savannah in twelve hours.

Anticipation adds lead to her foot, and she pushes past the fifty-five mile-per-hour speed limit. Signs for Savannah urge her forward. High on adrenaline and six cups of black coffee, she imagines her dream family's welcoming expressions. She cannot consider any reaction other than acceptance and joy. Any other thought would be too bleak.

Finally, as she exits I-95 to take Interstate 16 into downtown Savannah, the sky opens with a welcoming vastness. Staggered stripes of pink and blue clouds stretch out in front of her. Five white church steeples dot the skyline, and she smiles at their reassuring presence. Like a prospector, she is eager for the treasures hiding at her destination. "I'm here, and I'll be fine" she says aloud, half convinced that it's the truth.

As she turns onto Bay Street, ancient buildings escort her into the city. The sidewalks are a kaleidoscope of activity. She squints at the stark contrast of the sparkling sidewalks against the weathered structures. Everything seems brighter than New York. Large, multi-story hotels line the left side of the street, flanked by palm trees that reach prickly fingers toward the sun. Shutters held open by intricate iron scrolls adorn every window while thick oak limbs reach toward the sidewalks, dripping tangles of moss.

Down a side street, she spots one of the lush, green squares she read about during the weeks of daydreaming that followed the discovery of the letter. Lara tries to figure out which square it is. While waiting for her student loan check to arrive, she had memorized all twenty-one squares and their monuments, turning them into a song.

"Johnson sits on top of Greene. Wright makes Tomochichi queen. Telfair hosts the artist scene," she sings.

A sizable gray monument is barely visible behind an immense flowering tree. She cannot make out the form. Everything, including the horse-drawn carriage now two-car lengths behind her, makes her feel like she has stepped out of a time machine. Nothing is familiar. Her surroundings match the uncertainty of her identity. Moving backwards because of a few obscure lines scrawled on notebook paper verges on insanity, but it is a madness she is willing to explore.

Chapter 5

June 10, 1991

Moss drapes over the gravestone. On the ground, a branch tugs at her jeans. Stooping to make out the words on the nearly illegible stone, she places a piece of paper against the granite, rubbing it with a crayon to capture the name of the deceased.

Noting the dates of the fourth Pearce grave at Laurel Grove, she considers whether the stone will reveal her roots. So far, the only death records Lara has found at the library are six volumes of Savannah's *Register of Deaths* for 1896 through 1920. With visits to the eight Pearce graves at Bonaventure Cemetery under her belt, she remains focused on 1920. Florence Martus had been waving thirty years by then and cotton was still a commodity. Still unsure but determined, she pursues dead Pearces, searching each stone for a mention of cotton, the name Martus, or the Waving Girl's mother's maiden name: Decker.

Pearce could be either her birth father's or birth mother's surname. In her mother's case, the tricky part will be figuring out whether it is her maiden or married name.

Pearced was she by the cotton race that will never end.

It is possible that whoever penned the letter was a poor speller and that Pearced just means stabbed. The idea of the word not referring to a surname is too frightening to consider. Without the name Pearce, her guessing game soon crumbles into a heap of nonsense.

To cover all the possibilities, Lara searches two generations back, starting with the early 1900s, looking for a Pearce relative. Grave records are one certain thing in Savannah, as the city prides itself on grand cemeteries and accurate remembrances of its dead.

Lara steps back to look at the surrounding graves. Her squeal surprises her more than the voice that draws it from her.

"Who ya lookin' for?"

The deepness of the voice reminds her of an actor emoting in an amateur production of *Gone with the Wind.* She half expects to turn and find a mustachioed man in tails. The Tara moment fades as anticipation pulls her spine taut.

Standing at dusk in the graveyard, pondering the intentions of the person behind her, Lara considers running towards the car and chastises herself for the cavernous lack of protective forethought. The most dangerous items she carries are a ballpoint pen and a crayon.

Deciding to turn, she holds her pen like a dagger and suppresses a giggle. The man in front of her is crooked with age, as pale and fragile as a spirit. His eyes are barely visible beneath sagging years of experience, and he twists his neck awkwardly to face her. A cane supports his thin frame as he reaches out a hand in greeting.

As she has so often done since arriving in Savannah, Lara inspects his features, looking for a hint of resemblance. She tries to discern the color of his eyes. It's hard to make them out in the fading light.

In the dreams that visit her every night, it happens like this. A low drum begins in her head. Like a funeral march, its tempo is slow and solid, and the family of look-alikes marches into view, arriving simply and without emotion. Taking their places on a nameless street corner, they walk alongside her in perfect cadence. Their relaxed familiarity envelops her in safety. The nightly dreams make her feel like a part of something rooted. Her shoulder-length hair and emerald eyes become glamorous in the company of those who share them.

The old man's neat goatee and well-mapped face exude social standing. As she daydreams of the family that she hopes to find, he carries out his own patient appraisal, clearing his throat to break the silence.

"Looking for anyone in particular? I'm sort of an unofficial guide." He gestures toward the front of the yard. "Been comin' here since my baby boy died. Buried both wives here. These stones are old friends."

"How'd he die?" she asks.

"'Failure to thrive' is what they said. Called back to heaven, I guess."

Lara smiles at the mention of heaven. "Looking for Pearces," she says. "This is Stoddard Pearce. I'm looking for a Pearce from the twenties. Could've been in the cotton trade."

"Hmm, Pearce." The old man touches his chin. "Can't say I know any here. Been to Bonaventure? Everyone's got a ghost there."

"My first stop."

She eyes a slice of sky through the oaks above the stranger's head. The last hopeful rays of daylight fade to reveal a darkness she would prefer not to experience in a graveyard. Lara considers excuses that might get her back to the car while there is still light on the path.

"Ya know, cotton was sunk by the twenties. Boll weevil came 'round 1915, and bales took a terrible drop. Where ya from?" he asks, interrupting her excuse concocting.

"New York."

"Got any living kin in Savannah?"

"Think so," she replies. "Long story."

"Well, if there's one thing I've got too much of these days, it's time." He offers her a calling card. "Name's Artimar Pace.

Pleasure to meet ya. If you need any help with your ghost hunt, call me. I'm a retired snoop. Be my pleasure."

Artimar turns with an aching slowness and heads down the oyster shell path toward the cemetery gate. She shouts, "Thank you," and tucks the card into her bag, knowing she will not use it. The search is far too intimate to share.

Five years earlier, when Lara was just beginning her search, she had encountered the first of several private investigators. Clutching at secrets that did not belong to them, they were the worst kind of money-grubbers. Lara was living with her mother and had signed up for a monthly adoption reunion newsletter using her friend Maria's name and address in order to avoid uncomfortable conversations with her mother.

Behind the closed door of her bedroom, with pillows piled high around her head to keep her mother from hearing, she'd made the call, naively expecting a rapid reunion. The woman who answered was in a hurry and asked for two hundred bucks up front. "That's non-refundable," she blurted, without asking for specifics.

With money due for her high-school band uniform, two hundred dollars might as well have been two million. Lara had cringed at the investigator's icy detachment. "Don't you want my date and place of birth?" she asked feeling dismissed.

"We can discuss that once payment is made," was the answer. Her search was just another business transaction to the woman. What had started as a hopeful conversation ended with a decision to pursue the truth on her own.

Watching the old man's back fade from view reaffirms her decision to keep the search private. Lara grimaces at the idea of a stranger inhaling her secrets. Her mother would say that she is "getting her Irish up," and she would agree, if only she knew she was Irish.

Frustration moistening her palms as she moves towards the entrance, she rationalizes the reaction. Handing out business cards in a cemetery hardly seems a respectable pastime, even if the man has good intentions.

Finding real answers has been a lifelong itch that Lara scratches routinely with no relief. Every year, beginning at the age of thirteen, on the anniversary of her nameless birth, Lara had phoned the adoption agency to ask for a copy of her adoption records. For the first five years, the conversation was a useless carbon copy of the year before. The same social worker delivered the same raspy reply: "That information is private and sealed in the best interest of the child."

On her eighteenth birthday, armed with the foolproof argument of adulthood, she dialed the phone again, sure she would get a new answer. Mrs. Rothmeyer repeated the yearly response, prompting Lara to ask, "What child are you referring to?" The woman with a beyond-retirement voice said, "You, my dear." With a tone that only a teen could muster, Lara informed Mrs. Rothmeyer that at eighteen years old, she was no longer a child and the conversation changed.

The social worker stopped Lara in her sure-footed tracks, saying, "Your birth mother signed a document that assures her privacy." Mrs. Rothmeyer's reply made Lara wonder for the first time if her birth mother might not want to be found. The social worker's comment turned her birth mother into a co-conspirator culpable in the theft of her identity: a stark contrast to the selfless victim Lara imagined.

Even now, fully immersed in the physical reality of her Savannah search, Lara worries that her birth mother signed the adoption papers, hoping to erase her accidental daughter. Shrugging off the possibility, Lara remembers the letter, proof that her mother wants to be found.

Tugging off her gold jacket for relief from the heat and glancing at her tattered bell-bottoms, she considers the old man's offer. *Thanks, but no thanks, mister. I'm going to find my truth the same way I deciphered the note: all by myself.*

Chapter 6

June 11, 1991

"Yeah, Mom, it's beautiful. Nope, I'm not staying out late." Lara turns the alarm clock towards her to check the time. "Yeah, I know. I know. I have enough to get by. My room is nice." Lara frowns at the pile of clothing and fast food wrappers that surround the bed.

The inevitable question comes next, and Lara answers lightly, hoping to paint the picture of an extended vacation rather than a hopeless endeavor. "Nope, I won't be home for at least a week. It's so nice here, Mom. I'm actually looking forward to staying a little longer. All depends on what I find."

"Of course, I have enough to pay for the hotel. Remember, Ma. Bea got me a great deal." Lara hangs over the edge of the bed to grab the wallet she stows under the mattress each night for safekeeping. Opening it, she makes a quick estimation of the number of bills inside.

"Have you ever known me not to eat?" Lara's stomach responds to the prompt, and she checks the nightstand drawer for leftover blueberry Pop-Tarts from her convenience store stash.

"Yeah, I'll save enough for gas to get home." Lara peels back the wrap of the last pastry, waiting for a pause in the conversation so she can take a bite. "Please stop fussing....Are you crying? Come on, Ma. I'm okay....I love you, too."

The phone back in its cradle and Lara still reeling from the fresh-slapped feeling that accompanies conversations with her mother sans coffee, she relishes the first sweet bite of blueberry goo. She had been in the middle of the reunion dream when the ringing had woken her. Deciding never again to attempt a mother-daughter conversation before massive amounts of coffee, she looks at the clock with more focused eyes and realizes that the rest of the world is well into the workday already. It's Tuesday at ten a.m.

Guilty anxiety gurgles along with the digestive juices, hard at work on the morning confection in her stomach. Her mother's concerned voice triggers another mental reprimand about the insanity of spending the student loan money on the trip. The college funds should have been off limits, but it was the only way to pay for the trip. After the letter, nothing could have kept her from Georgia's first city.

Not yet motivated to leave the richly threaded sheets, she focuses on something other than finances. As a teen, her mother answered every door-slamming episode and break-up drama with the same instruction: "Find something positive to focus on, Lara." To avoid the lashing her blame-driven adoptee self is about to deliver, she begins a maturity checklist to prove the logic of the Savannah trip.

One…changed my major to English, so I'll have a chance at a real job after graduation.

Two…the trip is a learning experience.

*Three…*She cannot come up with a number three, imagining instead her mother, on her knees, praying for the return of her wayward child with loan money in hand.

"Come on." She rolls over, trying to find a positive, frowning when she spots her missing sandal wedged into the toppled ice bucket.

Okay…three…the research skills from the trip will be useful for a future career.

This would be true if Lara had a plan. She is clueless when it comes to a career path. More than once, her mother has reminded her that squeezing toxic, sugar-laden goop into fried pockets at the local doughnut shop is not résumé worthy.

Lara often questions if she'll become anything at all. All her life she has listened to cousins talk about goals in advertising and law, and as each headed off to an Ivy League life, her life tumbled deeper into a crevice of genetic failure. Instead of planning what to do, Lara spent year after year trying to figure out who she was. Even in Savannah, the possibility of a successful family seems unlikely. Genetic anti-heroes are easier to believe in.

Taking the only photo she has of herself as a newborn from her search notebook, Lara examines the infant's expression. Someone snapped the photograph at the hospital just after her birth. She asked Maureen Bonavito about it at the wide-eyed age of seven and her mother had said, "We're lucky to have it, Lara. They don't usually photograph babies who are given away."

The response brought with it the image of a trashcan filled with toss-away children awaiting distribution. Today, she knows it was probably just a slow day on the maternity ward and is happy to have it. The concern on her scrunched-up infant face makes her question if she had sensed what was to come and whether her mother had held her even once. Lara imagines a face beyond the photo's edge.

Lara speculates on how alike her two mothers might be. She believes they both love her, yet she constantly must make peace with the way they left her, the first physically, the second emotionally. Maureen Bonavito ditched high school to marry the monster and spent a decade in his hard hands. Now that she is free from physical danger, lack of education is her biggest enemy. Her life is a non-stop treadmill of work, addiction, and poverty. She lives in perpetual struggle and frustration.

"Enough!" Lara throws her legs over the edge of the bed, pushing away the bulk of the down comforter to escape the heaviness of her imaginings. Daylight streams through the drawn curtains as Lara considers the other mother whose name she does not know. Famous faces come into focus. Free to picture any birth mother she wants, she brings Princess Diana and Meryl Streep to the mental casting call. Lara savors the inexhaustible options of envisioning famous faces. Seeing her mother for the first time will plunder the fun possibilities, replacing them with what she hopes will be a healing permanence.

Neither mother is likely to offer her the iconic normalcy of a Norman Rockwell life. Yet, on soft-serve days like this, each receives a bath in symmetrical sweetness. Sugarcoated mothers make the search easier to continue.

Chapter 7

June 11, 1991

"Always?"

"I've always known I was adopted," Lara explains to the librarian who stares in anticipation of hearing more. Whenever she asks for birth or death records, the reaction is the same. The moms of the world absorb her story as if breathing in the scent of a newborn. The idea of deliberately ripping apart a mother and child at birth is unfathomable to them, so they ingest her story with empathetic eagerness.

Years of answering questions asked by doe-eyed women have given Lara insight into a biological relationship she has never experienced firsthand. When she mentions the search for her birth mother, tears run, faces melt, and shoulders lean inward as if to take up the position left vacant.

This morning, the librarian inhales her story, sharing her own climb up the family tree. "I think we discover ourselves in our history." The librarian smoothes a curl of hair as she speaks, recalling the relative from whom she inherited her auburn locks.

"How true," Lara agrees.

"One second, ma'am," the librarian interrupts to check out books for a teenage girl whose nails click impatiently on the counter.

While she waits, Lara ponders the librarian's comment. Lara will never get used to the way people disregard their history. They refer to family habits and familiarities just as they blink without any idea they are doing it. The non-adopted just know.

The librarian returns as Lara considers the gift of self-knowledge. The finger-tapping teen leaves, and Lara envies her ability to attribute her long legs to her grandfather. She longs for a source, for anything solid to pin herself to.

Lara engages the librarian again. "History's a part of who we are and the choices we make every day." Feeling generous, Lara bestows a few more morsels of her adoption. "I've always known I was adopted. My mother called me her 'beautiful, adopted baby.' Once I figured out that 'adopted' was different, I asked about it. She said I'd grown in a poor mother's tummy and that I was adopted to have a better life."

She stops there, not divulging the sinister fabric of her childhood. No one wants to hear about her dangerous placement. The librarian digests the half-truth, and Lara is proud to have protected her listener, as she examines the empathetic face of the recipient. The librarian points to the research section that Lara already knows holds the Chatham County *Register of Deaths*.

Lara looks around the church-turned-library that is her daily destination. Entering patrons pull at weighty red doors. Bookshelves stand in neat rows along the scarred floorboards where parishioners once shuffled along in their Sunday shoes. Her destination at the top level of the once-consecrated structure is a hushed research area, which used to be the choir loft.

Her search is tangible. It resides amid millions of words packed into microfiche and reference volumes. Instead of a flimsy plan, the books give her search a texture. Even paper cuts are welcome reminders that every word represents the possibility of blood relatives.

Opening the *Register of Deaths*, Lara paints mental pictures of the people behind the names. Every day since arriving in Savannah, she has searched for something meaningful in the finality of the one-dimensional entries, seeking to uncover what happened between the dates of birth and death. Lara knows that dates do not define human life. Yet, each has the power to define her.

Her graveyard visitor, Mr. Pace, suggested that boll weevils launched their first attacks on cotton in 1915, and he was right. So today, she turns to the year before the ruin, 1914, guessing that the "cotton race" had something to do with dwindling production and the greedy competition that follows most economic downturns. Tiny print, organized by date of death and surname, makes scanning each page monotonous, and after two hours, not one Pearce appears.

Lara yearns for the familiarity of home and the comfy camaraderie of a good talk with friends over a few beers. The charming shops, delicate manners, and moss-laden lanes of Savannah have yet to reveal a single fact. Yet strangers greet her on the streets with such familiarity that she feels as if they know her. It is so unlike the place where she molded her half-truth. New York is a whir of people scurrying from place to place. Savannah moves in a sunny, slow motion breeze. The letter suggests that this is her biological mother's home, but today Savannah feels foreign and lonely.

Lara lays her head on the table. She's looked through fifty-eight pages from 1914. The air in the library is heavy with moisture. Having ditched Greenwich Cemetery for the cool of the library, she hopes she hasn't wasted the day. Remembering the loan money and not wanting to fritter away even one minute that it buys her, she leaves the library as her most meaningful clue draws her back to its source.

The baby's roots are with the Southern lady who waves forever.

She is a large, bronze statue at the riverfront. Lara read about the Waving Girl at the Babylon Library before the trip

30

and later in a twenty-eight-page booklet purchased at a T-shirt shop on River Street.

Since finding the statue, Lara has wanted to know what kind of group would memorialize a desperate woman. Besides the family names and a general description of Florence, all Lara knows about the woman is that she waved at every ship that came to Savannah from 1887 to 1931 and that she loved and lost a man. The Waving Girl's romantic woes hardly seem worthy of eternal reminder. Savannah has salted the wound forever.

Lara decides to seek out human interaction downtown despite the ludicrous ninety-eight-degree temperature. She will ask real people about Florence. There has to be more to the story than a sprite of a girl waving at sailors for forty-four years. Lara cannot imagine doing anything night and day for forty-four years. Eating maybe, but beyond that…she wants to know what might inspire such resolve.

Passing a teahouse packed with a clientele of pleated ladies wearing shades of mauve, marigold, and persimmon, Lara considers the discomfort of asking locals random questions. Trying to figure out what she will say, she tests her opening line in a whisper, "Hi there, I think the Waving Girl is a long, lost relative. Bwahaha." Lara can't help but laugh at the oddball comment, and a couple of exiting teahouse patrons recoil from the outburst.

Sizzling like a steak at the devil's cookout, she stops first at a romantic little shop with lace-covered table displays and a massive wall of books. Inhaling the calming aroma of ancient literature, Lara looks for the shopkeeper or clerk. A kid with purple hair and tattoo-covered arms creeps forward from the back of the store. He looks like he just rolled out of bed. Knowing how she'd react fresh from slumber if a stranger squawked at her, Lara considers a quick browse and hasty exit. She reminds herself to be brave, and once the string bean teen plops down behind the cash register, she approaches him. "So uh, hi. I'm looking for information on Florence Martus."

The kid shrugs and takes a long sip of his Pepsi before answering. "Never heard of her. She from around here?"

"Yeah, well thanks. I'll just look around." Lara feigns interest in a few dusty books before leaving.

Her next stop is the air-conditioned antique mall on Bay Street. Surely, anyone who appreciates relics from the past should have some clue about the Waving Girl. Lara squints at the brilliant array of etched crystal vases, gem-colored glassware, and mirrors that greet her inside the store.

"Welcome, welcome." The shop owner's lean frame is perched atop a wooden stool sandwiched between two display cases. She looks at Lara over metal-rimmed bifocals hanging low on her nose. "Help ya find something?"

"I'm, uh…" Lara adjusts her weight from one foot to other and the floorboards whine. "I'm looking for information about Florence Martus, ya know, the Waving Girl."

"Our local loon," the woman laughs and puts down the roll of receipt paper she's been attempting to thread into the register.

"Excuse me?"

Looking like she has been waiting all of her earthly days to be asked this question, the slight woman stands and reaches out to shake Lara's hand. "Name's Harmony. Now, let me tell ya what I think 'bout our Waving Girl." Her face grows serious.

"She was a sad creature for certain. Poor thing hardly entertained a soul on that island. Florence was the lighthouse keeper's sister. How lonely she must've been living with that brother of hers in the middle of nothing."

Grinning ear to ear as she contemplates the splendid secret she is about to reveal, the shopkeeper wiggles her eyebrows, indicating the juiciness of the gossip bomb. "She met a man though. That sweet thing fell for a military man. Lord knows how she met him. His ship must have docked out there or something."

Harmony stands and leans a bony elbow on the case between her and Lara, resting her chin on a hand decked out with more rings than Lara has ever seen worn at one time. Lara studies the silver and gold trinkets that line the case below.

"Not sure when or why the guy left," Harmony continues. "Some say that's when she started waving. Never did stop. I heard that poor soul was a mess when her brother retired. They had to carry her off the island. Dementia likely. Don't blame her for going off the deep end though. I'd surely lose it if I had to live with my brother all the time. He drinks more than a cooter bug." The shopkeeper's laughter joins the symphony of brightness, turning the store into a bellowing assault on the senses.

"My brother would kill me for saying so." Harmony laughs again, and recalling her sales position, asks, "Did ya see our little Waving Girl statues? They're on the back shelf."

Lara looks towards the miniature statues as Harmony continues, "Sorry I don't have many details, sweetie. Might try the shops down on River. Someone there is bound to have a better take on her."

Thanking Harmony for her time, Lara leaves.

River Street is abuzz with tourists browsing, taking photos, and congregating outside Savannah's Candy Kitchen, where a divine smell lures Lara in the door. She stops to watch a large man plop buttery pads of pecan delight onto an enormous tray and looks for someone who seems approachable. In one of the thickest drawls she has encountered so far, the candy-maker asks, "Anything I can help ya find?"

"Actually, I'm looking for information on one of the local statues. You think any of the employees might know about the Waving Girl?"

"Hang on just a sec."

He removes a caramel-stained apron and slides the tray of buttery confections into a sweet-laden metal stand.

"Meet me in the ice cream room. I think this ol' boy can clue ya in on a few tidbits of that tall tale."

Lara moves aside to let a bunch of giggling teens grab praline samples from the marble counter.

When Lara first arrived in Savannah, she'd asked a greasy looking clerk at a gas station about the Waving Girl. He called Florence a prostitute, suggesting she entertained men on the island, "'cause it was the only way she could make money." Lara hopes the candy guy does not reiterate the gas attendant's sordid opinion. A beard and heavy jowls give the candy-maker the look of a ship's captain. He lowers himself with a sigh to sit behind the counter, gesturing for her to sit across from him.

"The name's Buddy Hartley. Yours?"

"Lara Bonavito, from New York. I'm sort of writing an article about the statue."

"Well, Lara from New York, seeing how you aren't from these parts, I'll back it up to the beginning. Sound like a plan?"

"I don't want to keep you from work," Lara answers, watching as a small group of customers gathers in the breezeway between the candy and ice cream rooms. Applause erupts as a toffee maker propels a batch of saltwater treats through a clear overhead tube from the kitchen and into a multi-tiered sample stand in the showroom. Tourists grab up the freebies, the littlest among them consuming the chewy sweets in a flash.

"Secret is, I'm not really working. I own the place. Let someone else get their hands sticky for a bit." Buddy tidies a pile of napkins on the counter as he talks.

"Thank you so much." Lara is relieved that this guy might actually know something.

"Been here my whole life and I even recall when they set her statue in place. Was the early seventies. I was in high school and they had some grand unveiling. She's been over there," he gestures to the right, "waving at our river ever since, but I'm guessing you want to hear more about the lady herself?"

Lara nods, hoping for new facts.

"Well then, Florence Martus was her name. She was long gone when the statue was built. Lived 'til forty-three or forty-four, buried at Laurel Grove. People say she was shy as a church mouse, but she sure was a doozey of a flag flapper.

"Florence was born on Cockspur Island out near Fort Pulaski. Loved them ships even as a kid, always watched as they passed her house. Father died when she was about seventeen. German, if I recall. Anyway, her brother got the job of lighthouse keeper and took Florence with him to Elba Island."

Taking a rag from under the counter, Buddy wipes down the silver straw dispenser as he talks. "Story goes that she met a sailor and fell in love. Never did see him again. He left with his shipmates, and that was that. So Florence took up waving. Guess she was hoping one of the ships would be his.

"Her brother told the newspaper that she kept that sailor's handkerchief up her sleeve, unleashing it at every ship until it plumb wore out. Replaced it with a kitchen towel, and at night used a lantern, making sure she'd be spotted."

Taking a single napkin from the neatened pile, Buddy wipes perspiration from his brow and continues, "Between chores she waved and the ship folks sure did 'preciate it. After a while, they started sending gifts, writing letters, telling everybody about the lady who waved in Savannah. Excuse me." Buddy interrupts the story to wait on a pig-tailed cutie standing at the ice cream counter, flapping two dollars at her sides like wings.

"Whatcha want, sweetheart?" he asks, holding up a finger to let Lara know it won't take long.

"Stawbarry kid cone pwease."

Buddy hands her the cone with a smile and asks Lara, "Want something sweet, New York? I highly recommend the Double Do Ya chocolate sundae."

35

Lara says no, but her mouth is watering as she eyes the little girl's already melting cone.

"So...where were we? Oh yeah, she was waving." He chuckles before continuing. "Well, Florence flapped something or other 'til her brother retired. Not much written about her after that. Except about a birthday dinner the city held for her seventieth. Lord, people came from far and wide, saying sweet stuff to that old gal. She was supposed to speak, but got all choked up an' couldn't do it.

"Her story was told over and over, and like most things in Savannah, it grew like a weed. They say she waved at one-hundred thousand ships, can you 'magine that. No surprise that ladies' club put up a statue. Pretty good hospitality, I'd say. You've seen it, right?"

"The statue?" Lara answers. "Sure."

"So you saw the old collie that lived with them on the island. Guess she loved that dog all right. Fed him from the table. Did I mention she was a grand cook? She'd be in the middle of cooking or gardening and always knew when a ship was coming.

"Here's a bit of trivia for your article, New York." Buddy's hands are busy again, filling a tray with white plastic spoons from a cardboard box. "When the statue was unveiled, the club put a dozen red roses down for her. My mama said a man from France sent the money with a note asking the club to buy them roses. Said he loved Miss Martus. Must have been an old coot. Always thought it might be her sailor."

Lara has been taking notes amid mounting disappointment. Nothing about the statue or Florence's life seems related to her.

"That 'bout wraps it." Buddy stands and comes around the counter. "Hope that helps with the article, New York. He smiles and pats her shoulder.

"Thank you so much. I really appreciate it. You've helped a lot." Lara's not sure that any of the information is helpful, but she knows a bit more about the Waving Girl. *Probably more than I know about myself*, she thinks, thanking Buddy again.

Chapter 8

June 11, 1991

Buddy said Savannah immortalized Florence because she made people feel welcome, like they were coming home. In front of the statue at Morell Park, Lara leans on a pillar, examining Florence's facial expression again. There is no joy. Her face is so solemn it is almost severe. Florence wears a modest dress that covers her neck to ankle. Staring at the handkerchief caught on a permanent breeze, Lara wishes for a hint of the long forgotten gust. Moving closer, she observes a spider spinning its web in the shade of the sizable bronze shoes. A dark lantern sits at Florence's feet.

Mystery teases her heat-constricted brain as she tries to decipher how the statue connects to her background. Examining the woman's close companion, Lara marvels at the detailed rendering of the alert collie, its mouth open and tongue extended in a panting pose. The woman and dog look out to the Savannah River through eight crepe myrtles that flank the walkway. Tracing the shape of Florence's dress with her eyes, Lara follows the lines past Florence's ample bosom to the full skirt and reads the inscription again.

Her immortality stems from her friendly greeting to passing ships, a welcome to strangers entering the port, and a farewell to wave them safely onward.

Few tourists come to photograph her. Circling the brick patio, Lara looks for clues beyond the dates 1869 to 1943. The club erected the expensive statue but failed to post Florence's story. With all the myths surrounding Florence's life, leaving the reason for her waving to legend must have seemed a safer option.

Lara's instincts tell her that the clue is not about Florence's family, but something else. Thoughts of Florence fly off, along with a startled mockingbird, as day becomes night. The Savannah River is bright one moment and ominous the next. The first time a freighter, carrying a five-story stack of shipping containers, inched its way past the statue, Lara covered her ears at the drone of the engine straining behind her. The immense ship obstructed the entire river with its cumbersome heft, an ugly invader amid the historic backdrop. This time, Lara does not turn to look at the eyesore of commercial goods bound for parts unknown.

Enjoying the slow-moving stretch of shade cast by the commercial ship, she opens her notebook to look at what she jotted during her chat with Buddy. The note and its suggestion of a familial link do not fit in Buddy's explanation of the Martus family and without a Pearce surname in the Martus family line, Lara remains more lost than found.

Her heart was Pearced and so was that of her mother.
Pearced was she by the cotton race that will never end.
Buried in the first city is a man who holds the 9th key.

Lara sequences the clues again, looking for a sensible story. If Pearce is a name and cotton race sets the years where should she look next? The ship's shadow leaves Florence's face, and the mercury notches up ten degrees. Woozy from thinking, walking, and pondering familial possibilities, she decides to take a break.

As the sun fully resumes its powerful position, she checks her wallet and is relieved to find she has enough cash to fund another trolley tour. With a week in residence, she'll learn more from a tour now than she did the first day. The tour she took when she first arrived in Savannah was awful. The tour guide suffered from mumbleitis and reeked of onions. In typical Lara fashion, she'd mentioned her less than stellar experience to the tour company and, in typical Savannah fashion, they had given her a half-price coupon for another try. A lack of leads, achy feet, and a heat index of one hundred and four degrees make this the perfect time to take advantage of the air-conditioned escape.

Chapter 9

June 11, 1991

Cash and coupon in hand, Lara walks to the trolley stand further up River Street. Waiting with a mass of tourists, she imagines where each resides. The bald guy with the NY Jets hat is easy. The Lucy look-alike with the purple polka-dot dress is harder to place. She examines the group, killing time before boarding and sitting at the back of the bus.

Lara watches a line of linen-suited men cross the street and pictures the men she has encountered in Savannah. Every Southern movie has at least one sweet-talking, well-dressed man, so she expected honey-coated manners and dapper attire but not the layer of frivolity below their correctness. Men of her age dress in clothing that varies as wildly as their occupations, while older male Savannahians dance between sinister and sultry with formal attire, precise shaves, and secure smiles. Being surrounded by beautiful women every day must polish their self-esteem.

Turning her attention to the tour guide, she is pleased. He is helping the last tourist aboard, holding her hand as she maneuvers the final step. He looks to be in his early thirties with bright eyes and a sexy smirk that opens to a smile revealing a few age lines. Lara recognizes a gracefulness in his mannerisms that she has only seen in men's aftershave commercials and the soap operas they interrupt. She settles in, looking forward to an entertaining ninety minutes.

She notices his well-defined muscles as he points to the iron balustrades covering the windows of the two- and three-story buildings that run the length of River Street. Housing sweet shops, an old-time photo studio, and a collection of pubs and tourist boutiques, the buildings boast an ancient assortment of bricks. Each facade wears a different shade of red due to the harsh sun, age, and damp demeanor of the city.

The guide presses the microphone close to his lips, making his breathing audible. His accent is enticing, not severe. He licks his lips between southern-spun words and Lara smiles.

"The brick buildings on your right once rang with the wheeling and dealing of cotton brokers whose offices were situated above the warehouses where they stored the coveted fluff."

He tells the stories of Savannah in hushed tones. If the words were just a tad different, Lara would think he was talking about a lover. He offers up each museum, monument, and square with romance and intrigue. "She's irresistible an' hard to get to know, but y'all have a ton of fun tryin'." He looks in her direction and she wonders if the tingle at the back of her neck is a reaction to the air-conditioning or him.

Lara is glad she chose the round-trip tour, instead of the more expensive hop-off option allowing visits and re-boarding at various historic sites. Enjoying the scenery inside the trolley is going to be fun. Her unnamed guide points to the Waving Girl as the trolley moves over the rough stones that pave River Street. As they head towards Bay Street, she watches his Adam's apple bob and considers how his skin might taste.

Geez, Lara. Are you in heat or what?

As they pass behind the Waving Girl, the nameless guide tells the most familiar version of Florence's story with romantic flourishes and flattering innuendo. In his telling, Florence is a lonely hero, her sailor a cad unaware of the grandness of the woman he left behind.

42

The trolley traverses more uneven pavement, jostling up a narrow roadway hardly large enough for two cars. The guide does not speak again until they pass the Davenport House. Before he opens his lovely lips, he pushes a stray hair from his forehead and Lara sighs. She looks around to see if anyone heard the audible admiration. Across the aisle, the American Gothic couple she pegged earlier as being from Wisconsin stares accusingly. Lara raises the free city map she has been using as a fan to cover her amused grin and attempts to focus on her guide's words rather than his physique.

As they pass a multi-windowed building with its two-sided entry staircase, he says, "Designed in the Fed'ral Style, she was scheduled to be demolished in 1955. Would've been lost if not for the seven Savannah ladies who saved it. Davenport was the first project for the Historic Savannah Foundation, and it ignited a preservation renaissance here. The women raised funds and bought the house in 1955. Savannah's historic crusaders were Katherine Clark, Elinor Dillard, Anna Hunter, Lucy McIntire, Dorothy Roebling, and Nola Roos. Those fine ladies saved my city one brick at a time.

"Notice the double stairway, ladies. It was created with your honor in mind. Men went up one side, women up the other. Since men were not supposed to see even an inch of exposed ankle on an unwed woman, separate stairways kept reputations safe."

Lara is clueless when it comes to architecture. Beautiful buildings make her scrutinize the people who built them. Her freak of an adoptive father was a builder and worked on New York's World Trade Center. She'd first entered the shiny spectacle of that building as a child and could not fathom how a man who dished out so much pain had managed to help create something so beautiful.

Lara makes a mental note to check out the courtyard garden the guide is now describing. "Behind many of the courtyard walls, you will find lush gardens and sitting areas. These are some of Savannah's best-kept botanical secrets." Lara cannot imagine any of Savannah being lost. She admires the seven women and the foundation they formed to save Savannah's secrets.

Forsyth Park is one of her favorite places on the tour. The fountain at the center of the park sparkles with pristine lightness. She sighs again when the guide looks directly at her and says, "If you like our fountain now, you should see her when she's knee-deep in green for St. Patrick's Day." Lara smiles a cross-eyed grin at the farm couple, who are glaring at her again. Lara pictures them posing naked in front of a barn with a pitchfork.

The guide's description of the immense crowds, beaded breast-baring ladies, and drunken joy that washes over Savannah on St. Patrick's Day has her hankering for a cold drink. Passing the golden window displays that kitty-corner Broughton Street, she considers getting off the trolley to shop. A small outdoor market tantalizes the senses with multihued produce and shoppers carrying mesh bags or wheeling larger bundles behind them in carts. She can almost smell the peaches ripening on street-side market tables.

From Bull Street, they head down State Street to Barnard Street, ending up at another square. The trolley pauses in front of a large building with five, life-size marble statues out front. The guide explains, "The Telfair Art Museum was designed by an English architect named William Jay. The big boy statues you see guarding the goodies inside are Phidias, Raphael, Rubens, Michelangelo, and Rembrandt. This square was Saint James Square until 1883, when they changed the name to honor the Telfair family. The Telfair Academy of Arts and Science, on your right, is a wonderful monument to a woman keeping things in order."

He wraps every Savannah site in a womanly reference. "Mary Telfair never married and when she died in 1875, left her home and furniture to the Georgia Historical Society with instructions that it be turned into a museum. She also specified that there be no eating, drinking, smoking, or amusement of any kind in the house."

Lara figures that the woman spent years arranging and maintaining the home and was simply laying down rules to make sure that no one messed it up after she was gone. A brilliant move in her estimation. What woman wouldn't want to keep things just the way she liked them for eternity?

The bells of Trinity Methodist Church greet them as they leave the square. The tops of the church columns and immense steeple disappear in the sky over the trolley as the guide purrs on, "Trinity Church is built on what was once the Telfair family garden. The church is the oldest Methodist church in my sweet city. The cornerstone of the church was laid in 1848."

Traffic and tourists crossing streets without the benefit of crosswalks slow the ride back down Barnard Street and Bay. The guide increases his volume, describing the monuments they pass. "We are now passing Emmet Park, named for Robert Emmett, an Irish rebel who led a rebellion against British rule in 1803. Poor Mr. Emmett, they captured, tried, and executed him for his efforts.

"Notice the Celtic Cross just ahead. It was erected in 1983 to recognize the significant Irish ancestry of Savannah. I am sure y'all have seen more than a few redheads crawling through the pubs on your vacation. He winks at no one in particular. Lara inhales deeply, admiring his eyes again, then looks away to study the large Celtic Cross and another small cement monument topped with a bronze eagle.

"The trees that shade Emmett Park are live oaks, and this row was originally an Indian burial ground, so watch out for ghosts if you take a stroll down here tonight."

The cardinal-red M of the Marque hotel sign is visible in the distance now. The idea of ending the tour saddens her. By the time the Waving Girl statue comes back into view, the tour guide has thoroughly charmed her. She allows herself a thorough assessment of the dimple-cheeked specimen she will leave behind for reference books. Lara thought she caught him smiling at her several times during the tour, but brushes it off as wishful thinking.

When the tour ends, she waits quietly for everyone to disembark. As soon as she is the only one left on the trolley, Lara shifts her skirt and re-tucks her blouse before approaching him. He is fiddling with the microphone and turns to her after setting it down.

"Thank you for a terrific tour. I learned a ton more than the first time I took it." The inane comment flares her cheeks.

"Really, when was that?" He cocks his head, leaning closer to speak.

"Last week." She fingers the button of her shirt, avoiding eye contact. "Your company was kind enough to give me a discount on this tour. I would've been happy to pay full price though."

"What brings ya to my city?"

She makes the mistake of facing him fully, and he looks her in the eyes. He studies her as if admiring a prized possession. Adrenaline kicks in, and Lara talks to suppress her nervousness. "I'm looking for family here. Been poking around cemeteries and libraries since I arrived."

"From?"

"Oh," she smirks, her cheeks still burning, "can't you tell? New York. The accent is usually a dead giveaway."

"Thought so, didn't want to be rude." He stretches his arms out behind him, clasping his hands behind his neck, as if settling in for a long chat. "I'm done for the day, and that's no way to see Savannah, young lady. Join me for a drink?"

He jumps from the trolley, skipping the steps, and offers his hand to steady her slower descent. A long line of tourists look at them, impatiently waiting to board and get some relief from the heat.

46

The guide is at least ten years Lara's senior and better looking than anyone she has dated previously. Lara shifts her stance to steady her mind and body from what feels likes an onslaught of heatstroke. Fanning her face with the trolley brochure she's had clenched in her hand, she answers, "Sure, I'd love to."

She stands outside the trolley office while he clocks out. When he emerges, her stomach pops like kernels on oil. Before college, Lara slurped hundreds of drinks with men who started as strangers, but something about it happening in an unfamiliar city makes her giddy. Smiling and willing her feet to move, Lara suppresses a giggle when a Christmas melody pops into her head...*put one foot in front of the other.*

He lifts an arm as if to embrace her shoulder and holds it there, a cloak of protection from the horde of tourists.

"Where are we going?" she asks, only mildly curious about the destination. She is much more interested in her nameless guide, whom she follows as steadily as a child hypnotized by a piper's alluring tune.

Lara's cheeks burn from the thrill of strolling down the street with a total stranger to a location known only to him. For a moment, danger warns, in a voice that can only belong to her mother, and Lara is reminded of the plentiful number of handsome predators she's seen on the six o'clock news. He could be taking her anywhere.

The guide's handsome features, the prospect of a real conversation, and the little creases around his bluest of blue eyes usurp the space where her mother's voice is booming, and the warning floats away as quickly as it arrived.

Chapter 10

June 11, 1991

The bar is three hundred yards from the trolley. It is a homey looking place with a mahogany bar and cushioned booth-style tables. As they enter, her guide winks shamelessly at the redheaded hostess and moves without hesitation to a vacant booth near the window.

She sits first and her stomach flips. His handsome demeanor makes her anxious, and Lara fidgets, sliding the silverware around the table.

"Before we order," she musters the courage to ask, "May I know my tour guide's name?"

"Robert William Taylor, at your service," he answers with a smile, reaching across the table to shake her hand. Her hand flops weakly in his. She was not ready for the shake, making it awkward. Like a puppy in training, she fails the simplest of tricks.

"Nice to meet you." Looking down as if caught in a lie, a wave of unfamiliar timidity crashes over her. Shyness is not an attribute Lara has ever heard associated with her name. In fact, people always comment on her boldness. Yet, Robert Taylor makes her feel like she's dancing naked in Times Square.

"So where ya staying?" he asks, wiping a tiny trail of sweat from a trim, stylish sideburn.

"At the new hotel at the far end of River. Really nice except for the people aquarium they call a lobby."

"No kidding, I've been there for a charity thing. They had a piano bar in the lobby. I remember looking up, imagining what we looked like from the balconies. We were in tuxedos while kids screeched and splashed in the pool thirty feet away. Nuts."

"What was the charity?"

"It was a local group that was raising money to restore a few old homes. So many houses in the historic district still need facelifts. Some need major overhauls. I don't point out any of the dilapidated places on the tour." He smiles, and she can feel the temperature in her face rise.

"The Historic Savannah Foundation raises money with fancy events, and then they buy houses, fix 'em up, and usually resell them."

"Lovely," she purrs. From the amused look on his face, she can tell that her tone was inappropriate and obviously not about the houses.

He reaches across the table again and touches her hand, asking about her trip to Savannah, her family, and college. They chat on, through a string of delicious mixed drinks, before he asks about her search for family.

The afternoon sun moves lower in the sky. They talk for more than two hours about their common status as only children, about politics, about Savannah history, about the abundance of mockingbirds in Savannah. Lara is more at ease, as her shyness melts to interest.

Robert is a native Savannahian and treats his tour guide duty as a hobby, not a career. He studied at SCAD, a private art college with a campus spread willy-nilly across the city. "SCAD stands for Savannah College of Art and Design," he explains, clearing up at least one confusing Savannah reference.

Someone had used a SCAD building as a landmark when giving Lara directions, and she was sure they said SCAB. She'd spent more than a few minutes contemplating what kind of organization would pick such an oozy moniker.

Robert attended SCAD to "keep himself busy." Throughout the conversation, he never mentions money. Lara can tell that it is a non-issue. He refers to his mother and father's home on East Gaston Street as a restored manor. The closest Lara had ever been to a mansion was when she hitched a ride and ended up at a party in a lavish, pink house at the seashore on Long Island Sound.

Lara laughs. "I've never heard anyone refer to their house as a manor."

The comment does not faze him. "My mother is heavily ensconced in the historical preservation of the city, so living in a restored manor is sort of expected. My father's in finance." Lara supposes that just means he's rich.

When Robert reaches across the table and covers her hand with his for a third time, she squirms. "Tell me more about your search?" he asks.

After a deep breath and self-reproach for the schoolgirl jitters now wreaking havoc on her body, she answers. Lara's voice squeaks at the onset of speech then settles to its normal timbre. "I was adopted in New York. My parents divorced when I was twelve. Bad scene. I always wanted to know about my real parents, but couldn't get much out of Mom. She said my birth mother was poor, and that's why she gave me up. I always wanted to see who I look like and who I act like."

Robert seems interested, so she continues, "When I was home from college last spring break, I found a letter about my adoption at my mom's place. It made me rethink everything. It mentioned the Waving Girl, someone named Pearce, and a cotton race." She's talking too much but telling him the story is a release.

Winding down, she adds, "So, I cashed in a student loan check, packed my bags, and here I am, searching a city that I never knew existed." Discussing the specifics of her search with someone in Savannah feels good.

Robert gives her hand a little squeeze. "Well, that's the most interesting reason I've ever heard for coming here, and I've heard a few." He sits back in the booth, removing his warm hand from hers, and an odd look of recognition and confusion comes over his face

"Wait a minute. Well, I'll be a..., have you been to the Chamber of Commerce? There's something there you need to see."

"At the old bank? What do you mean? I was there, just old offices."

His eyes sparkle with excitement, and for a minute, she believes he might be teasing her. "Come on, I'll take you." Robert pays the bill, and this time when his arm reaches around to cloak her, it rests securely on her shoulders.

Her feet ache when the two of them finally step up to the historic marker in front of the old bank building. Six massive cement pillars front the building and there is a brass historical marker in the portico. Lara figures whatever had sparked Robert's excitement must be in the text of the plaque and begins to read.

"I can tell you more than the sign." He takes her hand, pulling her through the large brass doors. "This is the Chamber of Commerce." She waits, expecting him to go off on a tour guide spiel. "I want to show you something in the lobby." He hurries, showing her the brightly lit area. "I spent a ridiculous amount of time here as a kid, and I can't believe this, really. It might fit into your search. What are the odds?" He is supercharged by whatever he is about to show her.

Inside, Robert asks the receptionist, an attractive mahogany-skinned woman, if he might show Lara some of the architecture. "Of course. Welcome to Savannah," she replies, sizing Lara up over the rim of her glasses.

With their backs to the receptionist, they face the corner of the lobby. Wooden racks block the wall. Robert and Lara squeeze past them toward a collection of historical markers set into the wall behind the racks. Each is beautifully illustrated and dated.

Lara can't understand why they organized the room so foolishly. The racks house a collection of tour pamphlets, restaurant guides, and hotel brochures yet block the medallions, each engraved with a scene that she assumes is from Savannah's history. While they're beautiful, they are not unique. Similar markers appear on iron fences all over the historic district.

Lara is woozy from afternoon cocktails on an empty stomach. She appraises her guide from the back, deciding that he is much more interesting than old discs. Robert kneels to point to one of the round medallions and she lowers herself, leaning on his shoulder to look closer. The medallion features a large bell and two words: "Pearce Cotton."

Lara nearly falls backwards. Pearce and Cotton. "I'll be darned," is all she manages. The words she's been looking for are right in front of her.

"What does it mean?" she asks, not really expecting an answer. "What is Pearce Cotton? Do they grow cotton?"

Robert waits a moment before answering, likely sensing the importance of the medallion. "When I was a kid, my dad was Vice President of the bank that owned this building. My mom used to take friends and benefactors through here. I sat here for hours." He points to a chair in the waiting area.

"Let me tell ya, there's nothing duller for a kid than spending hours cooped up in a stuffy ol' bank. I was bored out of my mind, sitting 'round waitin' and wishin' I was outside playing. To kill time, I memorized the medallions and created my own stories to go with them. That one made me curious 'cause of the bell. The only bell I can think of that it might refer to is the one that used to hang in the City Exchange.

"I tried once or twice in college to find out what each medallion referenced. Don't really remember lookin' up Pearce Cotton. Gave it a half-hearted effort, I guess, 'cause school got busy, and I forgot about it."

She takes in the characteristics of the building where this familial evidence has been on public display all her life, imagining a young Robert sitting below the antique yellow walls. Did he count the glass panes staggered across the ceiling, or the plaster flowers blooming at each corner? Her dream family starts a slow march around the plaster supports and down the barred floor-to-ceiling windows

Robert interrupts her thoughts. "Guess ya found the right guide this time, Miss Lara." He smiles and hugs her still stunned frame.

Robert explains the significance of the bell again. "That bell is probably the one that used to hang in the City Exchange building. They demolished the Exchange to build the new city hall. Some ironworks company bought the bell, and it was moved to a replica bell tower in the fifties."

Robert continues in guide mode, explaining, "The old bell was used during the 1800s to signal closing times for shops. It was also the warning bell for fires. They even rang it to welcome well-known visitors to Savannah."

"Where is it?" she asks

"Well now, I'll show ya," Robert answers, taking her back to the door.

Although her feet push forward, the minutes hang around her head with the intense humidity. Anticipation magnifies each step and echoes through a blossoming headache. Lara reflects on God's goodness as they start down the street. It is all so unexpected, impossible, and right.

They walk briskly, and she wants to lean against his six-foot frame. It is a familiar feeling, the reaching out for something solid to hold. A morbid, self-analyzer, Lara knows that being an adoptee and fatherless has carved a massive vacancy in her self-worth. With some awareness, but little self-control, she aches again to push someone into the empty space and take away the fear. As is her habit, Lara gives in, pulling

Robert closer, as they cross the street and head to the bell tower at Emmett Park.

Chapter 11

June 11, 1991

As they walk to the bell tower, Lara remembers the tribulations of New York. She cannot help but picture her adoptive family. Her mother will be devastated if she finds her blood relatives. Whatever else is missing between them, she knows that her mother loves her.

Erasing the years of criticism and dysfunction seems possible as she moves forward, arm linked with that of her handsome tour guide. Lara shivers with excitement. She has her first real lead. She prays it will fill the void. A therapist once explained, "You will try to fill the emptiness of not knowing your background with many things: some healthy, some risky, all futile."

Lara tries to assign a proper source to her giddiness. She is not sure if the quiver in her stomach is because of him or due to her progress. The difference between connection and attraction eludes her.

So cavernous was the lack of trust that formed her childhood that Lara seeks a bond with everyone. As a kid, the police officers and paramedics sent to end the violence in her evil dwelling became fast friends.

"Come and play?" she would ask the officers. She tugged at their sleeves, hoping for a smile instead of the inevitable mask of sympathy. For her, the violent eruptions brought hope. The flash of red and blue lights in the driveway and the abrupt silencing of sirens delivered calm. Her mother would be hauled off to the hospital for bandaging and encouraged to file a complaint afterward. She never did.

Her father would spend the night in a jail cell, and the resulting peace was a heavenly respite for Lara. Like the tranquility of an empty church, her home was happiest then.

Frequent police visits meant that Lara knew each officer by name. "Good evening, Officer Smith. Would you like to play Monopoly?" Like the memorization of her home phone number, knowing their names was a safety net.

Lisa from the Safe Haven Shelter for Battered Families was the first to squash Lara's naive image of the rescuers. Lisa had listened as Lara described the angelic friends who showed up in response to her mother's cries for mercy. Lisa replaced childhood fantasy with truth, saying, "The police and paramedics are not your friends, Lara. They were simply doing their jobs."

At first, Lara did not believe Lisa. Doing so would have erased her only respite. Just as she had expected the screaming, kicking, burning, and punching, she counted on the police for hope. Their pressed uniforms and spit-shined shoes were Lara's only reassurance of outside normalcy.

Ultimately, the escape had nothing to do with the rescuers. It was Lara's recurrent begging that won her freedom. At eleven years old, she'd confronted her mother after school. "Mom, I'm leaving if you don't."

Thought out in simple childhood terms, Lara's survival plan was to take the Long Island Railroad to the city and live in one of the box communities she'd seen there. Lara explained the particulars of her plan to her mother, showing her the few dollars she'd saved up for train fare. A new resolve emerged in Maureen that day, and she clung to Lara, crying and promising to leave the monster.

On the first day of summer break, Lara helped her mother pack everything they could fit into the back of the red Ford Maverick, and Maureen drove to a payphone at the Pathmark grocery. Months earlier, her mother had found the phone number on the bulletin board posted next to index card ads for cars and lawn maintenance. It read, "Abused? Need help? Call (800) 621-4673."

Lara had said farewell to her fifth-grade friends the day before. For them, the end of the school year meant summer fun and graduation to middle school. Knowing that she might never see them again and queasily dreading her unknown future, she mourned each friendship. Her best friend and neighbor, Laurie, teased her for the seriousness of her hugs and tears.

"See you tomorrow, silly."

A single phone call found them shelter. Her mother spoke in hushed tones on the payphone at the busy market. The voice at the other end told her mother to go to Flo's Coffee Shop on Fifth Street and to look for a lady in a blue baseball cap. That woman handed Maureen a map with a red path drawn on it. At the end of the line, someone had drawn a big red heart.

They drove in silence for more than an hour, hugging the shore and heading east on Long Island. They passed the biggest houses Lara had ever seen. There was no indication of what they would find at the heart place, but her eleven-year-old imagination saw a castle with an ocean blue pool and circular drive. Lara was embarrassed when she considered how their compact car would look in the midst of such grandeur.

Approaching their destination, Lara's heart sank. Heart Place was a one-story, dilapidated motel. Grungy and unwelcoming, the motel screamed poverty with its tattered shutters, broken sidewalks, and an algae-laden pool. In front of the low building, sunken-eyed women sat in plastic chairs flanking numbered doors. Some of the doors were open and Lara heard the squeals of playing children. Many of the women chain-smoked cigarettes, lost in thoughts of the delicate balance between survival and death. Only one of the women seemed to notice the Bonavito family's arrival. She raised a scarred arm, pointing them to the office. They learned later that Mimi's elbow-to-wrist scars were the result of hundreds of cigarette burns inflicted by her mobster husband.

The room they were assigned had a double bed, sink, single burner stove, mini fridge, and groaning window air conditioner. Lara lived at Heart Place for an entire summer, learning about the other monsters that roamed the earth in the form of men. She came to love the motel for its silent walls and secure locks.

Every family at the shelter got a social worker. Lara's assigned counselor was Lisa, a beautiful, soft-spoken newlywed. During their first meeting, Lisa used smart social worker words to make Lara feel lucky. It was the first of many shiny new adjectives that Lisa would apply to Lara. Lucky was something Lara never considered herself. In fact, the only luck she associated with her life was the bad kind.

Daily counseling sessions gave Lara a less prickly perspective on her pre-pubescent life and the predicament of hotel homelessness. "This place is for lucky kids, Lara," Lisa had said. "Many women do not survive the abuse, and their children end up in foster care."

Two weeks of listening to the stories of the other shelter families convinced Lara that living at Heart Place was a blessing. She was safe but bored. The children's activities scheduled that summer were infantile, and the three TV channels they watched in static frustration ran endless reruns of the *Price is Right* and *Merv Griffin*.

Lara escaped the dull reel of shelter life by reading well-worn romance novels borrowed from other residents. When she thought she could not abide another sweaty male torso, Lisa presented her with a copy of *Jane Eyre* by Charlotte Bronte. Lara devoured the book, finding solace in Jane's shared loneliness and brave withdrawal from Gateshead. A kinship grew with every word, and the previously dull nooks and crannies of Heart Place burst with heroic, romantic, and tolerable possibilities.

Recalling the good fortune of that summer, Lara picks up the pace, in a hurry to gather whatever evidence waits at the bell tower. She hopes to find an answer there. The tower looks too small to hold a bell of any significance.

Robert stands back, sensing she might want to be alone. While she reads the inscription at the base of the bell, Robert considers why he picked her. She approached him, obviously flustered and pretty in a northern way with busy eyes and broad gestures, and he was intrigued.

Having headstrong parents who talk endlessly about heritage and ancestral pride amplifies Robert's interest in Lara. With a lineage he can trace back two hundred years, Robert finds it hard to envision not knowing one's own heritage. Blood is everything in Savannah, and Lara does not even know her own mother.

Moving aside to let a man in a wide hat pass, Robert pictures his mother, whose ambition earned her a leadership role in Savannah's reconstruction. His mother's rigidity makes him curious about the softness of women like Lara. Dating for him is a casting call of vulnerability and supple congeniality, traits lacking in the jackal he calls Mother.

When Lara asked about his parents, he referred to his mother as a storm trooper. "Always ready to swoop in and solve a crisis," he said. Picturing her in full combat gear and sipping a respectable cocktail, he laughs. Lara turns, to see what Robert finds funny, and instinctively checks her boots for trailing toilet paper. He shrugs, wiping Military Mom from his mind. Lara turns back to the inscription that describes the bell.

Robert finds the uncertain tone that punctuates Lara's determined words alluring. She is blissfully easy to read. Never before has he heard anyone speak openly of being adopted. In Savannah, not belonging to your bloodline is a secret worth keeping. He has certainly never met a woman gutsy enough to spend college tuition money on a trip to a strange city alone.

Lara finishes reading and looks at Robert again. A tear moves down her pale cheek.

"You okay?"

"I need to go back to the hotel. My head's pounding, my feet are killing me, and this is too much. I need to write it down and think."

He moves closer. "Would you like me to walk you to the hotel?"

"Nah, I'm a big girl. I'll be fine." She wants to be alone. A storm of hysterics is brewing.

"May I call you tomorrow? I have a morning tour. I could buy you breakfast."

His eyes focus intently on her, and his warm expression makes it hard to resist a cry in his arms. Laying her mystery on his wide shoulders and taking him back to the hotel would be easy, but she cannot afford to add another link of regret to the chain of one-night stands forged in college.

"Yes, room two-O-seven. The Marque on the River. About seven o'clock?"

"I'll see you then. Sure you're okay?"

She walks away so Robert will not see her weepy expression and answers, "Yes, thank you so much...for all of this."

Chapter 12

In a perfect world, every man Lara fell for in college would have been a mindful match instead of a place to hang her insecurity. Robert is a marvelous guide and a much-needed distraction from the monotony and loneliness. He might also be a handy deflection of her need to fit snuggly into someone's world.

Beyond his physical appeal, Robert has already helped with her search. Trusting her instincts around men is impossible, and that is why she left him at the bell tower.

Lara rubs her brow, overwhelmed by the revelations and emotions of this day. It is way too much to process. Sitting at the edge of the hotel bed, she finds comfort in the notes she has scribbled since arriving in Savannah. She flips page after page, through the wishes, hopes, and findings that fill the three-subject notebook, until levelheadedness returns.

What does the bell mean? What about the marker? Has she been looking at the wrong years?

Lara does the math. Since she is nearly twenty-one, her birth mother was probably between sixteen and twenty years old when Lara was born. She uses the age eighteen as a starting point. If her birth mother was eighteen when Lara was born, she'd be about forty years old now. So, her biological mother would have been born around 1952 (give or take five years).

Dropping the pencil and pacing the few steps from the desk to the hotel bed, she contemplates a life paved with guesswork and assumptions. All she wants is one solid, unquestionable fact. She looks up and asks, "Is that really so much to ask?"

She must find out how the Pearce family relates to the bell, and more about the medallion. She can assume that her birth family was in the cotton business at some point, maybe in 1915, but why would they get a medallion in the bank, and why does it have the exchange bell on it? Tomorrow, she will have to figure out what "Pearce Cotton 1915" refers to and how it relates to the search.

Pearced was she by the cotton race that will never end.

Lara lies on the bed, staring at the popcorn ceiling, considering the significance of the Pearce medallion and how the Waving Girl fits in.

Pearce Cotton, a race, the exchange bell, and the Waving Girl are her jigsaw puzzle pieces. The Waving Girl was long gone from Elba Island by the time Lara's birth mother was born.

"Wait!" she yells at the flowered wallpaper and leaps up to grab the Savannah tour book she purchased at a souvenir shop on River Street. Flipping again to the dog-eared Waving Girl page, she finds the date. They erected the statue in 1972. Her mother would have been about the right age at that point. Maybe she visited the Waving Girl statue and left a clue.

Ridiculous. Lara knows every inch of the statue by heart and there is no reasonable place to stow away a clue for all these years. Then the idea hits. Perhaps, her mother's story is the same as the Waving Girl's. The one constant in Florence Martus's story is that a sailor came to port, loved her, and left. Her father could be a sailor. The Waving Girl clue could be her birth mother's way of telling her that she waited for him and that he never came back.

Pulling the bedcovers to her chin, she tries to figure out what direction to take next. Sleep beckons, yet just as her body begins to relax, she is jolted awake by the image of Robert pointing to the medallion, all smiles, so engaging.

Tangled and twisting under the covers, she gives up on sleep and takes a hot bath. The water trickles against her skin and she continues to think of Robert, imagining what he is doing and whether he is thinking of her. She recalls his excitement about the medallion and the way he stepped back to allow her a first look at the bell. As she dries her appendages, she decides that Robert's excitement and reaction were charming. Two acetaminophen and a medicinal rum and coke later, she is asleep and dreaming of Robert and the many ways that he might guide her.

Chapter 13

June 11, 1991

What time is it? Lara wakes with the sick feeling of not knowing where she is. The room is dark except for the alarm clock, which she has moved to the desk across the room. A slice of light from the balcony door reminds her that she is at the hotel. Laying her head down on the pillow at six o'clock was supposed to clear it, not send her off to la la land without dinner.

Her stomach is screaming now, and it is only eleven o'clock. In New York, the clubs are just starting to move and shake, and here she is awakening from a four-hour power nap. She snuggles deeper into the bed, bargaining with her hunger for a few more minutes of leisure. Hunger wins, forcing her from the coasting calm. She dresses quickly, cakes on some makeup, and grabs her bag.

The hotel restaurant is no longer serving, so her only option is the lobby lounge where a semi-circle of seats surrounds a large television. At least there is something to focus on while eating. Lara feels awkward eating alone in public. People stare, and waiters pity your solo status.

Sucking in her gut, she chooses a barstool close to the lounge chairs and leather couch. A perky blonde with a flip hairdo shows up. Beneath the syrupy sweet "May I help you," Lara spots disgust at the idea of anyone requesting food this late at night. She orders the fattiest midnight snack on the menu—

cheese nachos, and the bartender twirls her eyes in horror, before scurrying off to place the order.

By the time the piled-high plate arrives, Lara is drooling. She dives in with ravenous enthusiasm so hungry that even as she gobbles the nachos, she contemplates what desserts might be lurking in the lounge kitchen.

The bar is empty except for a woman dressed in a too-tight, blue satin dress. The heavy scent of sweet gardenia wafts from the slouching figure. With one hand propping up her head and a plump elbow on the bar, the satin doll watches an endless thread of weather forecasts on the TV.

Grabbing the last laden chip, Lara considers asking the waitress why Savannah clutters up the newscast with a weather report. Since her arrival, every day has been the same. It is always hot and humid with a chance of thunderstorms. It would be far more sensible just to record the forecast once and replay it every day in June.

Wiping cheesy leftovers from her face, Lara turns to discover that the place is not as empty as she thought. In a lounge chair, at a corner table, sits a dark-skinned man with a long beard and posture so straight he looks like he might be wearing a brace. He smiles when she glances at him, revealing a gold tooth.

"May I see a dessert menu?" she asks the waitress, as the familial and romantic possibilities of the day come back into focus. She is second-guessing the timeline she chose when decoding the letter. The Pearce graves she has visited are all of the cotton era, but her birth mother's era seems more sensible. The records for recent years will be easier to find, but the medallion was about cotton. Changing the focus of the search frightens Lara, almost as much as what she might find when she unearths her biological connection to Savannah.

Searching among the living would be much easier on her nerves. Every bird chirp and wind gust sent her heart into a panicked flutter in Savannah's cemeteries. Even in daylight, they're spooky places.

Yet, she has to look at the past for material about the bell and Robert's Pearce medallion. The idea of more library time makes her yawn. The server has left the dessert menu in front of her, along with the bill. Hint hint…Lara signs with her room number, praying she'll have enough to cover the splurge at check out. She stands to find the dark-skinned man beside her.

"Welcome to Savannah."

Lara nods and starts to walk around him.

He moves to block her. Her heart drums into wary action.

"I saw you with Robert. Be careful. He chews tourists up and spits 'em out. 'Specially pretty young gals like yourself."

"How do you know Robert?" she asks, barely masking her indignant surprise. She is aggravated that this guy was able to sneak up on her, and concerned that she did not notice him.

"I watch all the goings-on on River. Dance with the ghosts so often that the living rarely see me. You didn't notice me when you came in. Did you?"

Creeped out by the stranger's approach, with the nachos pushing all of her sleep buttons, Lara craves the warm bed that waits for her upstairs.

"You might want to listen to what I have to tell." The man does not sound like a Savannahian; his accent is cleaner, with just a touch of twang. He picks something from his teeth with a long pinky nail and holds out his hand, inviting her to his corner table.

"No thanks." Lara rises again to leave.

"Did he show you his medals of dishonor at the Chamber yet?" The stranger says it loud enough for the server to hear, and Lara decides he must be hard of hearing.

The comment has earned him her open-eyed attention. Lara cringes at the kind of crazy that might inspire this stranger to follow her and Robert. Why would he bother? As long and thin as a willow branch, his infectious grin settles her nerves and she decides to listen to his story.

Lara points to the stool next to her and he sits. His clothing is too heavy and youthful for his bony frame. He wears a quilted amethyst jacket, slim black pants, silver boots, and a thick, gold ring with the initials AB.

"Would the lady bestow a bit of libation on an old fellow?" he asks.

Lara has never heard anyone refer to a drink as a libation. It sounds like something a knight might say in the Middle Ages. "Sure," she says, calling the waitress over to let him order. He orders an Old Granddad on the rocks with a twist of lemon. He takes a sip as Lara waits for him to explain how he knows about her and Robert.

Her stomach rolls as the midnight snack settles. Sleepiness has left her though. The "medals of dishonor" comment released a sock-full of adrenaline, and she wants answers. Could Robert be a creep?

She retains her composure by pretending to slip into TV zombie-hood, staring at the news. Contemplating the "medals of dishonor" comment, she decides he is talking about the medallions, but cannot figure out what the guy finds dishonorable about a collection of dusty wall decor.

He sips his drink slowly, extending that insanely long pinky nail, like a queen taking tea. Finally, after imbibing half the booze, he speaks again. "Robert may be a paid guide, but he's no historian of any account. For him, history is a tool to make women swoon. His family has more gold than the English crown, so he's got nothing better to do."

The reference to England makes Lara spit out the water she'd ordered as a diversion, and she laughs. The pinky pointing, Old Granddad character is comparing Robert's family to royalty. The thought lightens her cautious mood, and the man introduces himself.

"Abel Bloom at your service," he announces with a dignified bow. "I have a flower shop near East Bay. Been there for twenty-eight years…came south in the sixties. Got tired of being the darkest thing in my home town," he says, chuckling infectiously.

"Where's home?" Lara asks.

"Canada, way up. Only a handful of black folks on the rock. My grandparents ended up there as hired-help, came by ship with a Welsh family from England. I'm the first to get away. Left 'cause of the snow. You know it's too cold when the polar bears start creepin' in on icebergs. Can you imagine that? What you think they'd do on River Street if a polar bear strolled by?"

Lara laughs again, and the furry image washes away her initial trepidation.

"I ended up in Savannah 'cause me bones needed warming. Got as far south as me legs and cash would take me. Would have headed to Florida or some island if I'd not run out of gas and money.

"Took to making palm roses when I got here. Thought I was saving for more travel. Have you seen them, made from palm fronds?"

Lara nods. She purchased a palm rose from a River Street rose peddler the day she arrived in Savannah. Initially woven of two fresh, green palm leaves, the rose had dried to a rigid, straw color in its safekeeping spot above the hotel room mirror.

"Well, I made those beautiful buds and sold 'em for a dollar or two. Made tiny bouquets of them in shell pots I marked Savannah. The tourists couldn't get enough of them."

"T'wasn't long before I was making five dollars a shot. The roses and work at the sugar factory kept me fed, so I stuck around. Plenty warm here, more like a melting pot than a warming spot some days."

Able continues, "The tourists liked my stuff, so I started making keepsakes from anything I could scavenge. Old Marvin

Stillbauter up on Broughton Street bought a couple of my creations and put 'em in his shop. They sold right quick and I made a pretty penny off 'em. Who can account for the fathomless folly of the public? Old Kip had that right. Anyway, that's how I saved enough to open my shop.

"Now, tell me your story. I know you're looking for someone or something in Savannah. Just sorry old Robert found you. Rudy claimed that the female of the species is more deadly than the male, but I'd have to say, after watching Robert, old Kip was wrong."

"How do you know Robert?" Lara asks.

"Well, these digits are getting too crippled to keep my shop open all day, so I have plenty of hours to spend on the river watching tourists come and go. Old Robert's taken more than a few young ladies to the bank."

Abel tsk-tsks and shakes his head before continuing, "After the third or fourth time I saw the bloke saunter to Molly's with one of his girl guests from a tour, I followed a bit, and his next visit was always to the Chamber. Kipling said he only knew six honest men, whose names were What, Why, When, How, Where, and Who. Good bunch, that group.

"Thought it strange how Robert had a date after every tour, so I followed him. Free country, so I watched him take one of his little sparklers inside the old bank. She was from up north, like you. Saw him circle the reception desk and Yolinda gave him a wave. Yolinda's been working there for a basketful of years. Listened to her chat up the young lady while Robert snuck in the lobby. He pulled a disc from his coat and put that thing on the wall. All around were others like it.

"As soon as the young lady rounds the corner, he points at the wall, saying, 'Here it is, just the way I remember.' Now that gal looks like she'll cry. Slick Robert puts his arm around her and smiles. After they left, I see ol' Yolinda take up the disc, sliding it in her desk. It made a racket as she slid it in, clanking against what must'a been others. I hung 'round to butter old

Yolinda into sharing a bit of info. Didn't have a blessed clue what Robert was up to until Yolinda yapped like a retriever. Seems Robert enjoys some pretty perks. Perky northern perks mostly."

Abel smiles again, and Lara taps her foot nervously against the bar.

"The way Yolinda tells it, Robert shines up to any pretty young gal who tours alone. He picks the ones with the most questions. The more they ask, the more likely he'll choose 'em. After the tour, he heads to Molly's where he digs around in their heads for some needful thing. Everyone's looking for something. So, Robert digs for a family name, a secret, a memory, and invites his ladies for a private tour the next day.

"When they meet up, Robert has a disc ready for Yolinda to put up, or he puts it up himself while Yolinda yaps. Robert's quite an artist, you know. Couple of his oil paintings are up at Gallery 209. Mostly of rich folk's houses, but he has a pretty nice bust of Robert E. Lee there, too. One Robert to another, I guess. Well, when all is said and pickled, Yolinda gets a fast ten bucks and Robert gets an ingratiated young lady."

Lara is silent.

"I know you're thinkin' twice about this old bird telling you this. But I saw last month's gal getting in a cab down here in tears after her twist with him. Not right to act like an old rooster in the chicken coop. That poor thing looked just about as sad as if she was at my shop ordering funeral flowers. So here I am, warning you."

Lara is beyond confused; the Pearce medallion cannot be fake. She saw it with her own eyes and only met Robert on the tour. Like a television detective working the world's flimsiest case, Lara decides that Abel's insinuations are false. What could Robert possibly gain?

"I don't know what to say." Fumbling with her purse and tapping harder on the bar with her foot, she considers the angles. Her mother gave her the angle speech before she left for college.

"Consider the angles, Lara. Life experiences are as different as people are. Nothing is absolute. Try to see what the other person sees. Don't jump to conclusions. You'll be much happier for it."

Now Lara considers why this old man might want her to think that the medallion is fake. Is he trying to get back at Robert for something? Could Robert really have created it for her benefit? There was no time, was there?

Abel gulps down the last sip of whiskey and stands. "Well, my dear, I told my tale, and now I'm gonna stroll home under the cool canopy of our starry Savannah sky."

Still not sure of anything, except that the man next to her doesn't seem to have a reason to deceive her, Lara reaches out her hand to shake Abel's. Feeling the cold of the heavy gold ring he wears, she says, "Thank you."

Abel smiles, showing off a gold-capped tooth and hands her a business card with a foil rose and script moniker. It says "Abel's Bud and Blooms." She takes it, says goodbye, and stares again at the tacky plaid jacket worn by the TV reporter.

Her head full of sleep and sadness, Lara decides that Abel's damning observations are cause enough to call Robert in the morning to cancel breakfast. Her day will now begin with a trip back to the bank to look for an empty spot where the Pearce Cotton medallion was. If it's gone, she will know that Abel is telling the truth.

Chapter 14

June 12, 1991

Lara picks up the phone to call Robert at six-thirty a.m., pausing to question if Abel was a vivid dream brought on by the lard-laden midnight snack, probably wishful thinking.

Her hand trembles as she dials. She clears her throat to rehearse the conversation. The seductive timbre of his voice makes her reconsider the decision.

"Good morning. How're you feeling this beautiful day?" he asks.

"A bit under the weather. I'm going to have to beg off on breakfast."

"Oh no, I'm sorry. Anything you need? Want to try for dinner?"

"Umm, better wait and see how I feel." She wants to scream into the phone and tell him how happy she is that she didn't invite him to her room. He is calm and sounds concerned. Lara seethes at the idea of a tour guide taking advantage of the very people who keep him in business.

"How about soup or something to eat? I'd be happy to play delivery boy."

"No, thanks. I'm going to rest."

"Okay. I'll check on you later."

"Goodbye, Robert. Thanks." *For nothing?*

Robert stands in his bright kitchen, perplexed. Lara did not sound sick. Smoothing his thick hair, he removes the sport coat he donned to take her to breakfast. Picturing her alone in the hotel room, Robert is at first aroused, then worried. He reminds himself how different she is from the others. She seems accustomed to being alone.

Fiddling with the coffeemaker and looking for a filter in the cleaned out pantry, he curses his housekeeper's constant reorganization of his things.

Finding what he needs on the top shelf, Robert recalls the moment that Lara mentioned Pearce and cotton. He was certain Miss Yolinda had spilled the beans, sending Lara to blackmail him for a few more bucks. The chances of her mentioning a marker that actually exists are astronomical.

Robert cannot recall when the replicas became a habit, but he finds them easy to make, and they have certainly spiced up his life. Connecting with women on the tours frees him from the boring socialites his mother is constantly introducing him to. Whenever she calls to invite him to dinner, Robert can be sure that a single woman will be there.

Anxious to halt her endless matchmaking, Robert tested the waters with several of the prosperous pretties. Conversations consisted of endless gossip about other socially prominent families and Savannah social events. The only thing worse than their chatter was the reputation-mongers they called mothers. They dressed their daughters in form-fitting designer duds and then pretended the little vipers were nuns.

Barbara gave him an angry earful when she discovered that he was no longer a reputable option for Savannah's upper crust of single women. His habit of returning precious daughters well beyond any respectable hour, often at dawn, turned out to be his undoing. Robert shrugged it off, moving on to a crop of moderately financed and infinitely more interesting outsiders.

Robert spent an inordinate amount of childhood hours in the lobby while his parents attended luncheons and meetings.

The time introduced him to the historical markers. The bank and his father's staff were his au pair. Imagination was his only companion, and he used every inch of its vividness to create dramatic stories to accompany every scene depicted on the wall. Unlike the lonely sepia of his childhood, the made-up tales were multihued and unbound by place or truth.

The lobby was his childhood slice of Savannah's beloved architecture. The medallions were as close as he could come to the importance of his mother's restorations. Each metallic canvas inched him closer to the fabric of her world. Transforming rubble into something to be adored for generations was essential to her, perhaps more significant than her son. Robert tries to remember when he first delved into the comfort of giving away historic connections. He is unable to recall the year, but the petite features of the first tourist he took to Molly's are seductively clear. With a wish tucked into her Savannah itinerary, the young woman was easy prey. That day and every time since, he found their secret wish. Every one of them craved something to connect them to Savannah's charm.

Walking along ballast stones laid a hundred years ago as a path for artillery and horses, tourists gulp in the chivalrous culture of his city. They need to own a piece of it, and Robert does his best to help them take possession. The gifting of Savannah began with a casual mention of the marker menagerie to the brunette from California. Sympathy filled her almond eyes as he shared lonely childhood memories.

Robert escorted her from trolley to lobby, sharing imagined tales, and she touched the markers, inhaling their boyhood significance. The deeper he waded in the shallows of made-up tales, the closer she swam into his arms, and a mutually ideal process was born.

The next one stayed four days, giving him plenty of time to provide her with a real connection. Who better than a tour guide to bond people to a city?

The first switch took the longest.

In the attic of his parent's home, Robert dug out a box of iron extras, leftover from a restoration at Factor's Walk, the series of concrete walkways and iron railings that run parallel to the Bay Street side of the cotton warehouses. His mother oversaw the replacement of six, precious frieze medallions on the walk, and thanks to Robert's artistry, each was a perfect recreation of the original.

"Never know when we'll need them again," his mother said, before asking him to haul them up to the attic. The box held twenty-six metal discs, all the same size of those in the bank lobby.

With a touch of molding clay and paint, Robert created the first disc for Mary from New Hampshire. Mary told him of her grandfather's sailing excursion down the East Coast on a schooner, and how he'd crafted a flag with a star for the four cities he loved most. Her grandfather wrote to the city's mayor, explaining how the people and hospitality touched his heart. Grandpa Teddy planned to return to Savannah but died before he got the chance.

Robert filled that first medallion with a flag of four stars unfurled across a calm seascape. Heading to the lobby the next day, before their scheduled meeting, he secured the marker to an empty casing.

It was a perfect fit and despite the others jutting out a tad further than his artwork, it looked like it belonged. He informed Mary over breakfast that he had found something she might enjoy.

She was awestruck. The idea of a permanent depiction of the flag was eerie. She cried when Robert showed it to her. She wondered aloud if her grandfather had shared the flag design in his letter to the mayor.

Mary was grateful and gloriously giving that day. She thanked Robert in ways he had previously only imagined.

After Mary, it became routine. Like leaving a gift for the mail carrier at Christmas or tipping an exceptional waiter,

Robert was compelled and comfortable, lifting both spirits and skirts. It was a steady stream of satisfaction for all.

When Lara mentioned Pearce Cotton, he nearly choked. She spoke the words, and an image of the marker came to him, as clearly as if he were standing in front of it. It was the city bell and the words "Pearce Cotton." He looked around the bar to see if the wait staff seemed amused. They didn't appear to be in on it.

Taking Lara to the bank was different. Showing her the marker made him feel important, genuine. It felt like a divine introduction.

Washing down the disappointment of the cancelled breakfast date with a chug of OJ, Robert thinks about Lara and when he will see her again.

Before yesterday's trip, Robert had not been to the bank in a month. While the dozen or so women he'd taken there made life less predictable, satisfaction dwindled with repetition, and none of the women contacted him afterwards.

Only Sarah from Milwaukee returned to the lobby to find the empty space where her marker should have been. After each excursion, Yolinda stashed Robert's creation in her desk. If the cleaning crew ever knocked one off the wall, his mother would hear about the damage. Yolinda covered his tracks for a mere ten bucks a disc.

When Sarah discovered the empty spot on the bank wall, she'd questioned Yolinda, who smiled halfheartedly and shrugged her shoulders. Crushed, Sarah discovered that the marker was as fake as the tour guide who'd taken her to bed.

The memory of Sarah's disappointment makes breakfast even less appealing. Sipping a cup of semi-warm coffee, Robert thinks of Lara's trembling vulnerability as she stood at the bell tower, and wonders how he might help her. His mother is always full of advice. Grabbing the cup, he heads down the narrow stairs to call her.

"Good morning, Robert darlin'." Barbara is delighted to hear from her only son.

"Mom, I have someone visiting, and they're sick. Staying at the Marque. Any ideas for a nice pick-me-up?"

"Well…I'm guessing this friend is of the female persuasion." She does not let him answer. "It is about time, Robert, you're getting a little old for the bachelor artist nonsense."

Without so much as an inhalation, Barbara Taylor goes on, "When someone gets sick, the society uses a little place over at City Market, Abel's Blooms. They do a 'brighter day basket' with flowers, pecans, fruit, and other goodies. I hear they're gorgeous. Better hurry though. Abel closes at noon. Huh…, hold on, son."

Robert fidgets, waiting on hold for three minutes. He is accustomed to interruptions and to being the silent party in conversations with his mother.

Itching to hang up, he paces. His mother would never stand for it. He considers telling her that he was disconnected. Tapping the telephone table impatiently, he remains on the line.

"Sorry, kiddo…got to run. Call me tonight. Let me know how it goes with the girl. What's her name?"

"Lara." It is the first word he has uttered since his opening question.

"Lovely. Bye, son."

As soon as she hangs up, he calls the flower shop. It could be just the thing to seal the deal.

Chapter 15

June 12, 1991

Lara takes her time showering and dressing. She is not anxious to prove that Robert is what Abel described. She needs the Pearce Cotton disc to be on the wall. There were no family dreams last night. She dreamt of Robert. *You sure can pick them,* she chastises herself, praying that her first impression of him will hold up.

Making a few Pearce calls seems a sensible start to this potentially volatile day, so Lara begins with the first Pearce listed in the Savannah white pages.

"Hello. J. Pearce, please."

"Yes, ma'am, Brother Pearce speaking."

The man's intonation makes it immediately clear that he is black. Trying not to be impolite, she explains, "I'm looking for relatives named Pearce who lived in Savannah in the 1960s."

"Now, child, do I sound like yaw kin?" the man asks, laughing.

Lara chuckles. "I didn't want to be rude, but thank you."

She dials the next Pearce. No answer. Three calls later, she has left a message, suffered one rude hang-up, and laughed along with the non-relative. She crosses three Pearce names from the phonebook, deciding that she has made enough calls for one day.

An image of the medallion hangs in her head, like a coin in mid toss. Heads, it is real. Tails, it's a miserable fake. It has to be true, yet the odds feel like they are stacked against it.

Walking to the Chamber building is like swimming in a sweat suit. It's only a few blocks away, and she walks, hoping the activity will help her burn a few ounces of the late night nachos. Lara passes the bell tower, pretending not to see it. If the medallion is not real, the tower means nothing.

As she enters the Chamber building, the receptionist from the day before, smiles at her vacantly. Lara ignores her and turns to the racks of tourist brochures. Pretending to search for a specific leaflet, she looks around to make sure he's not there. Kneeling in front of the lobby wall, it takes less than a second to find an empty space where Robert could put the fakes. Her heart beats faster.

There are at least a dozen medallions around the empty spot, but the Pearce medallion is on the lowest section of the wall, all the way to the right. Touching it gently at first, then firmly, she wiggles it to see if it is loose. It does not budge, and Lara feels the telltale indentations of the artwork. It is authentic, and existed long before Robert.

Grinning, Lara feels the forward momentum of the search return. She'll have to be cautious. Someone is lying, but she does not know whether it's Abel or Robert. The empty circle is there, but her medallion is as real as the surprised look on the receptionist's face.

Pearce Cotton is a bona fide clue. "Amen, amen, amen," she exclaims, a tad too loudly and winces at the echo that booms through the massive room. "Amen." She says it again as she passes the accused, conniving receptionist on her way out of the building.

Shoulders back, she strides pridefully through Savannah. The city is linked to her DNA. Savannah, once a stranger, is now a partner in the search. With a new sense of purpose, she wiggles into her hatchback in the hotel lot and eases past heavy pedestrian traffic to head back to the library.

Renewed energy permeates the return to her research. She has a tangible subject to search for in the card catalog. Pearce

Cotton is real, and Lara is ready to find out what it means. Joyful and excited, she cranks up the radio volume and sings along with Billy Joel.

At the library, she jots a list of topics for the day: City Exchange Bell, Pearce Cotton, and any court cases that have to do with cotton. Finding the company named Pearce Cotton would be helpful. Lara is enjoying the tracking of bona fide clues much more than guessing.

The Savannah Chamber building was built for Hibernia Bank in 1906. Did they place the medallion then? It was there when Robert was a child. That would have been in the 1960s.

Lara looks at the first few pages of the notebook for the Waving Girl dates. The statue was erected in 1972. Lara was two years old. She imagines her real mother standing in front of the same Waving Girl statue. Who built it?

She flips through the well-worn notebook for notes on the Waving Girl statue. The plaque at the statue said that it was the Altrusa Club.

She has to find out more about the club and whether they had any connection with a cotton race or the city bell. Her brain feels like a fried egg popping in a too-hot pan. In just one day, she has gone from no facts to more than she can fathom.

There is an entry in one of the library's reference books about the club, "The Altrusa Club of Savannah was founded in 1938 to serve as the local branch of the national organization. The Altrusa Club is an organization geared toward professionals who wish to engage in public service and foster personal achievement. Originally a club for women, the organization is now open to men."

Who were the members of the club in 1970? She will look it up, and hopefully, there will be a woman named Pearce.

Back down the choir loft steps, Lara asks the librarian where she can find a roster of Altrusa Club members for the period when they erected the Waving Girl statue. The librarian suggests the *Savannah News* on microfiche from the 1970s. The archaic machine used to view the film is a royal pain to use, but the photos make it worthwhile. Lara loves looking for some resemblance in Savannah's faces. Scrolling through the months preceding the statue's unveiling, she spots a brief club announcement. "A temporary chapter president and secretary were elected on the twelfth day of March 1970, due to the unexpected departure of Marianne and her daughter Virginia Senton. The Altrusa Club and historical commission are grateful for the Sentons' tireless efforts to preserve Savannah's historical gems, as well as their organization of the Florence Martus, Waving Girl statue, project."

Lara opens her notebook and writes the names Marianne and Virginia Senton.

The date on the announcement is a little more than nine months before her birth. Could they be her relatives? It is possible that her mother was a member of the Altrusa Club, but that does not solve the mystery of the Pearce surname. Lara considers the myriad of reasons why the Sentons might have left the club. "Oh my God." Startled, she stands, covering her mouth. "What if she was pregnant with me?"

The baby's roots are with the Southern lady who waves forever.

Grabbing her notebook and purse, she exits the skinny aisle of mammoth microfiche machines and is out of breath when she arrives at the front desk.

"Did you sign the microfiche back in?" The woman behind the desk whispers the question as if protecting Lara from the embarrassment of being untidy.

Lara hurries back to the machines, sticks the roll in its box, and signs the blasted paper. Hurrying again to the desk, she smiles as sweetly as possible and asks, "Can I get a phonebook?"

"Those are housed in current reference. To the back, all the way to the right."

She barely thanks the woman, who shakes her head in disapproval as Lara runs to the location of the phonebooks. Lara is anxious to see the Senton name in print.

In the roll call of possible birth surnames, she has created hundreds of options, changing them at whim, saying them aloud, signing her name with each one. Is this her family name? Softballs bounce in her stomach. Finding the phonebooks, she grabs the Chatham County edition.

Sepine, Sering, Sertin, Seth…she flips the thin pages. Her finger moves down the page that starts with Senator. Like tugging at a taut fishing line—she cannot wait to see what's hiding at the end. On page 444, she finds "Senton, Robert and Ann, Senton, Melissa, Senton, V., Senton, Barnard."

There are only four listings. Lara keeps the book close to her heart. This could be it. Of course, the odds are astronomical, and it is most likely pure happenstance. Adoption searches rarely end with such ease.

Still hugging the phonebook, she digs in her purse for a quarter as she heads to the copy machine near the entrance. The cover wobbles as she places the book on the glass. She makes two copies, just in case. She prays again, thankful for renewed hope.

Hunger pangs and the need for a private phone send her back to the hotel. She wants to make the calls at a decent hour. Three o'clock seems a little chancy. Most people work and aren't home yet.

Chapter 16

June 12, 1991

Bursting into the lobby, she sees him immediately. Robert is sitting in one of the leather club chairs, dressed in a perfect polo and crisp, well-fitting jeans. His legs are crossed, and he is reading a newspaper. He looks up once, eyeing the front desk.

Unsure whether to speak to him, sneak past the desk, or run back out the hotel door and re-enter from the parking garage, she stands transfixed as he turns towards her. He's spotted her. There is no way out.

Robert looks relieved to see her out and about. Her cheeks are flushed, and the muscles in her face tense as he approaches.

"Hi there, just coming to check on my new friend." Robert smiles and she feels the familiar tug in her stomach and other more pleasurable places. She wants to blurt out what she's discovered on this marvelous day but remembers Abel and stops herself, trying to think of an explanation for her wellness. Robert reaches forward to touch her forehead. She leans into the touch and accepts the embrace that comes next. It is longer than the farewell embrace they shared at the bell tower. As the hug opens, her stomach utters an entirely audible growl.

He laughs. "I hope that's hunger and not lunch returning."

"I'm starved," she announces, embarrassed by her body's musical display.

"Well, you must be feeling better. Would you join me for a late lunch?"

Robert looks blissfully at ease in his lovely skin. Between hunger, excitement, and the lunch decision she is now contemplating, she fears she might upchuck on his lovely Italian loafers.

Lara recognizes Robert's shoes from a top-ten article she read somewhere. She recalls being curious about what kind of men wear eight-hundred-dollar shoes. Now she has an answer, sort of. Lara has quite a few questions about Robert's intentions. She assumes that Italian cobblers don't base their designs on handsome artists who play at being tour guide to woo women with cuckoo history games. Yet, here he stands in their spiffy shoes.

Robert watches her stare at the lobby carpeting, swaying like a metronome. He reaches for her hand and asks again, "Lunch, dinner, something?"

She loves his hands. Tidy nails stand out against tanned skin. His hands have a muscular look of strength. His grasp tightens ever so slightly and she answers, "Sure."

They head to the main hotel restaurant. She feels underdressed for the dining room with its elegant linens, pink napkins, and crystal water glasses. He pulls out her chair and allows her to sit before sitting across from her. The host announces, "Linda will be your server. She will be with you directly."

Directly is exactly what she's worried about. What will they talk about directly? Should she call him on the medallion deal? How will she look at those eyes and keep from doing a nosedive into the porcelain plate?

They order, and the conversation kicks off exactly where they left off on the phone that morning.

"You seem to be feeling better. I'm glad. How horrid to be sick in a strange city. I understand you're not wanting see me this morning. I'm nearly a stranger, but I'm happy to bring anything you need."

Lara makes a significant and rare choice. She will let him do most of the talking. The quickest way to discover if he's just a bit off base, or completely certifiable, is to let him talk.

Robert clears his throat, and she watches his Adam's apple bob deliciously. This leads her eyes down to the lightly scattered, brown hair barely visible beneath his collar. She continues her downtown tour and is surprised at how still his hands are on the table as he speaks. Southerners never move their hands in conversation. Lara has no idea how they manage it. Hand gestures are a significant communication tool at home. With the level of sound at some Bonavito family gatherings, gestures were the only way to figure out what was going on.

"Would you like that?"

Uh-oh. She was letting him talk and had not heard a word he said.

"Sorry, daydreaming. What was that?" Lara looks up, avoiding direct eye contact.

"Would you like to come with me to see a great blues band tonight? They're playing at Mercury's. Do you like the blues?"

"I love the blues. My favorite is Buddy Guy. I saw him a few times in New York. He puts on a pretty wild show for an old guy in overalls." Lara smiles at the memory.

"I can meet you here at eight," Robert suggests.

"Sure, that'll give me time to change clothes," Lara says, surprised that she agrees so easily.

"Nothing too fancy. Don't want to make me look old."

"You're not old. Are you?"

"I'm thirty-one, unless you want me to be younger," he teases.

Eyeing him sideways through her bangs, she smiles.

"I love the blues, too. My parents listened to classical at home. Public radio was a nightly ritual. Dad read the paper, and Mom drank martinis, listening to university radio every night.

Not a bad thing," he continues. "I learned about current events and the sports that weren't popular in school. I credit public radio with my fencing fascination."

"Fencing, like sword fights?"

"Yeah, helps me keep in shape. We have a club here in Savannah. Nothing too formal, but it's my one addiction. I get to the community center at least once a week."

"Do you wear the whole get-up?" Lara licks her lips, which have gone dry from the image.

"Guilty as charged. Jacket, britches, helmet, the whole uniform. Have you ever seen fencing in person?" Robert asks. "You might enjoy it. I let my parents come to see a match once. They popped in after a city meeting. Mother was thrilled; thought it all quite chivalrous. She started calling me 'blade' as a joke."

It sounds chivalrous to Lara too. She imagines him dressed head to toe in tight white garb with sword in hand. Geez, all he needs now is a stallion so they can ride off into a propped-up, cardboard sunset.

He's talking again. The quiet chick thing is working.

"Ya know, my parents never came to my games in high school. I was no prize athlete, but I played baseball and soccer. Imagine them waiting until my twenties to lay eyes on one of my sporting endeavors."

"They never came to see their kid play ball?"

"No. Mom was busy preserving Savannah's historical integrity, and Dad was busy planning other people's fortunes and securing his own. Straight, narrow, and focused was his mantra. A good father...just a little distant."

Lara senses that the topic of his parents is a sore one for Robert, and his mention of historical work conjures up her latest clue, so she changes the subject. "Have you ever heard of the Altrusa Club?"

He looks at her and his face relaxes. "Sure. I think Mom partnered with them on a few restoration projects."

"What? No way."

Bingo, another link falls into place. His mother can tell her about the club and any connection to Pearce Cotton. Maybe she'll know why the Sentons left the club in 1970.

"My birth mother may have been a member," Lara blurts it out, wishing she could shove the words back in. She has to be careful. Robert may be more than a one-trick pony.

"You found more facts about your family?" Robert asks.

"Well, I'm not sure. I found out that the club erected the Waving Girl statue in 1972. I was born in seventy."

"Hell, I'm a robber of cradles."

Lara brushes off the attractive assumptions in the statement and keeps on talking.

Like a spider running from an eager boot, she continues, "I found a news article that mentioned two members leaving Altrusa Club in 1970. They were officers, same last name. One of them might be my birth mother. An unwanted pregnancy could certainly cause a hasty retreat from such a respected, upper class club. Don't you think?"

"Sure. We can visit my mother tomorrow, if you like. Maybe she'll remember something about all that. I'm sure she knew a few Altrusa members, and she's always happy to meet my friends. Gives her hope that I'm not a social pariah."

"I'd like that." Lara's heart gallops. His being a pariah is still something to consider. Robert's connection to her story proves stronger than the caution. Tomorrow's meeting might help her understand how the letter, cotton race, and Waving Girl are connected. The search is taking baby steps forward, and she is thrilled to have stepped from the purgatory of standing still. Robert's mother may hold all the answers.

In a delighted state, she allows Robert to take her hand. Despite carefully avoiding eye contact, Lara senses electric admiration and dangerous possibilities. Whatever he's done with other tourists, he's key to her search, and she is not ready to let him go, yet.

Leaving the restaurant, he continues to hold her hand, as they move toward the elevator.

"I'll meet you in the lobby at—" Lara turns to say goodbye and Robert places his hand at the back of her neck, pulling her to him for a kiss. She responds, the touch like a drug, a familiar elixir of healing.

Inside the elevator, the doors shut behind them, and they continue to kiss. Lara presses herself against him, seeking to seal the space between them. They stop kissing just long enough for Lara to unlock the door to her room. Robert is behind her, a hand at her hips, and his lips at her neck.

Inside the hotel room, she kicks aside the accumulated pile of clothing, hoping he does not notice. Robert does not seem to see anything except her. Still close behind her, he whispers, "Look at me, Lara."

She knows that if she looks him in the eyes, there will be no turning back. A small part of her is afraid to release the passion that she has given away so haphazardly in the past, yet she aches to taste him again.

Different from before, this physical need is not a bandage for her lack of identity. Making a choice beyond the subconscious crutch of neediness creates an unabashed feeling of abandon that urges her forward. More than physical attraction, Robert is an integral part of her search and connection to Savannah. Lara wants all he represents.

When she faces him, he takes her chin and lifts it to witness that she too feels the need. Her eyes tell him that she does and he kisses her more deeply, his tongue exploring, seeking to know. He moves his hands from her face and down the small of her back, pulling her gently against him so that she will know his excitement.

She releases the breath she is holding, and he smiles when she kisses him harder. Robert's hands run across her blouse front, caressing, and unbuttoning slowly.

He lifts her to the bed and she kneels before him on the deep mattress, reaching to remove his shirt. He helps her. She runs her hands through the hair on his chest and kisses him lower.

They are naked, intertwined, and sated when she forgets the search completely. Insecurity and the desperation of previous physical encounters fall away as he pushes her to release.

Lara wakes alone and naked, her clothing littered like fall leaves across the rug. As she sits up, Robert enters from the balcony, fully dressed and beaming. "Good evening, beautiful."

Surprised by his sudden appearance, she pulls the covers higher. Robert sits next to her on the bed. "Still up for the club?"

Feeling oddly embarrassed, she answers, "Sure, now get back out there, so I can get dressed."

Chapter 17

June 12, 1991

A familiar vibe greets her at the club. College students and a surprisingly young crowd play darts, pool, and shuffleboard. The place reminds Lara of the bars near her school. She looks for an open seat. Robert has other ideas. He nudges her towards the stairs, and they enter a much darker space with zebra-print stools and walls covered with autographed rock posters, musical instruments, and tattered stage clothes.

The upstairs crowd is older, and the room has a crooning Rat Pack vibe. They luck out, finding two seats at the bar as a couple gets up. Lara eyes, with parched appreciation, a giant martini sipped by the gray-haired man next to her. A picture of Abel and his raised pinky pops into her head, and Lara dismisses it. If she thinks of him, she has to consider what he revealed and what she has allowed to happen with Robert. Instead, she asks Robert about the drink.

"Biggest martinis in town," he tells her. "Like them dirty or fru fru?"

"Real martinis are too strong. Cosmos are good though."

Robert orders a dry martini for himself and a cosmo for her.

The band's singer steps to the microphone, and the guitar player fingers a progression of bluesy chords. The cosmo warms her stomach, and the music lulls her into a blissfully relaxed state. She lifts her glass and toasts Robert. "To finding." He seals the toast with a vodka-rich kiss.

Robert chats with the bartender about baseball, and Lara watches an older couple swaying on the dance floor. The man sitting next to her leaves and the woman who takes his place catches Robert's attention. He checks the woman out, licking his lip as if anticipating a juicy steak.

Lara shifts uncomfortably on the colorful bar stool, his obvious appraisal of the woman triggering a mental replay of Abel's warning.

The woman is older than Lara and looks like a redheaded Wonder Woman. Lara gets why Robert is looking at her. She is flawless. Lara starts to spin the barstool away from the statuesque woman when the redhead flashes a genuine, toothy grin and asks, "Hey, girl. How ya doing?"

"Hi." Lara smiles back.

While Robert returns to his conversation with the bartender, Lara strains to hear the woman over the music.

"I'm Susan." The woman introduces herself, proceeding to talk a mile a minute, using the most flamboyant language Lara's ever heard. Susan peppers every sentence with "girl" and "girlfriend" in an endearing Southern slang.

"Where ya from?" Susan asks.

"New York," Lara replies.

"Girl, don't miss the Pink House while you're in town. To die for...scrumptious. Not as scrumptious as that man you've got there, but tasty just the same."

Robert looks at them. He heard the compliment. Susan extends her hand to him in greeting. Much to Lara's unease, he kisses it.

Lara's eyebrows narrow at the *Casablanca*-esque spectacle. She just slept with the guy and here he is kissing the hand of a woman who is as flawless as a porcelain doll. Sun, pollution, and general decay do not appear to be on Susan's life agenda.

Lara gives Robert a slightly pissed-off look, and he whispers in her ear, "Just sticking to the Southern code. No worries."

Lara nods at the Southern code comment, but can't help but picture Robert's lips on all those tourists' hands.

Susan, who has refocused her energetic attention on Lara, is explaining the precarious path she took to become a successful interior decorator in Savannah.

"Started with a ton of inherited cashola and lived in high-cotton digs near Forsyth 'til mah dead husband's kids came crawling. They claimed that property faster than a hound'll suck an egg!"

Lara laughs at the image. Beyond animated, Susan continues, "Sold the place off and moved my pink palace to a condo. Course, I about fainted when I eyed the first mortgage bill. Then my son dove into a messy divorce, and I said bye-bye to my money."

This woman talks more than a New Yorker, Lara realizes, amazed by the personal details Susan is sharing with a total stranger.

"Five years, three months, and two days after my upscale lifestyle died with Everett, God bless 'im, I was flat broke, and started selling custom drapery for a high-end shop. My take was ten percent.

"I saw the world's tackiest decorating tragedies and could barely scrape a dime off my bills, so I turned designer. First clients were the Barneses. I sold them their window treatments and, girlfriend, they had the dither to make me rip 'em down when they hired me to redecorate. Now, if things get any busier, I may have to hire some help. You available?"

Despite Susan's daunting beauty and Robert's obvious appreciation of it, Lara likes her enough to share her story.

Keeping it short, Lara explains, "Not really, I kinda have my hands full. You see, I came to Savannah because of a note found in the family Bible. I'm adopted, and the note was about my biological family. I think my family is from Savannah, and I'm pretty close to finding them."

Tears well up in Susan Fletcher's eyes, and she hugs Lara hard, declaring, "You poor thang. I'm going to help you. We'll start tomorrow. Don't want to hog up all your date time." Susan lifts her chin to indicate Robert. "He's a keeper."

Susan writes her number on the back of a drink coaster and asks Lara to do the same. Susan downs the last of her drink and leaves after explaining her need for a "regula' ten hours of beauty sleep."

Lara pictures her sprawled out in a hyperbolic chamber lined with pink satin and lace.

Lara believes she has finally found a female friend. Despite the romantic greeting, Robert has not interrupted her chat with Susan, instead watching baseball on the overhead television. He touches her shoulder occasionally, reminding her that she is not alone.

Lara leans against Robert now, and they listen more intently to the band. The burnished bass and steady rhythms soothe her, as does the rise and fall of Robert's chest against her back. A calm possibility of belonging blankets her.

Chapter 18

June 12, 1991

Robert greets the hotel parking attendant like an old friend. The woman leans out from the attendant's window and hugs Robert, inspecting Lara with an amused smile.

Lara fidgets, realizing that the attendant might know about the medallions.

Robert's character and the revelations that may come tomorrow swim in her head as she listens to the easy pace of Robert's conversation. He seems honest. Meeting his mother should shed light on the true level of his sinister capabilities.

Lara kisses Robert goodbye in the lobby. He is eager to join her upstairs, but it is two o'clock in the morning, and Lara needs the perspective and space of sleeping solo.

In her room, a red button on the phone indicates a message is waiting. It has to be her mother. She listens. "Where are you, Laaaaaaaaarrrra?" Her mother's voice is clearly agitated and then softer, she says, "Please call me. I'm worried sick. I'm off tonight. I saw a robbery on the national news. Was it was near your hotel? Call me, no matter how late you get this."

She calls back, knowing it will not take too much conversation to placate her mom. Maureen answers on the first ring. She is sleepy and concerned.

"Thank God. Where've you been? I thought you were robbed. Did you see the news?"

"No, Mom, I didn't see it. I was at the library. Sorry I missed your call. I fell asleep when I got back."

"The library? Lara, it's two o'clock in the morning. You're still in the same time zone, right?"

Lara ignores her mother's sarcasm, crossing her fingers to void the lie. "Libraries stay open late here."

"Well, when will you be home? Have you found anything?"

Her mother is worried about more than the money. Lara knows that Maureen feels threatened by the possibility of another family.

Lara answers vaguely, "Nope, no real progress. Still poking around. A few leads, but no real progress."

"How much longer will you stay, Lara?"

"At least a few more days. I don't really know, Mom. You better get some sleep."

"I know, but you really need to figure out what you're doing. You only have so much time and money, and so far, it's a waste."

There it is, Lara's nightmares spoken aloud.

"Not a waste, Mom. Goodnight."

"I love you, Lara. Please call me tomorrow."

"Love you too. I will, Ma. Love you…. Bye."

Her mother assumed the trip would take a week. Lara has no deadline, except the one imposed by money.

Kicking off her shoes, she is happy that she did not invite Robert up. She needs to think. As a little girl, when the house would explode into an uproar, she did her thinking in the hall closet. There, beneath long wool coats and the soft tan leather of her father's rifle case, she dreamed and schemed for hours.

Escape plans, divorce plans, and questions about her real family came alive in the narrow hiding place. In a confinement of hope and hurt, she prayed her real family knew nothing of

95

her adoptive father's constant abuse and that they were searching to save her.

On particularly violent days, Lara would take her father's rifle from its case and consider the repercussions of using it on the monster. The possibility of a permanent end to the pain was tremendously attractive. Once, when he was watching TV in the family room opposite the closet, she'd aimed the rifle at him through the thin slot in the folding door. "Boom," she'd whispered, unable to pull the trigger. The image of filthy devil claws on the barrel and knowing that she'd burn in an eternal fiery hell stopped her.

The mirrored doors of the hotel closet remind her of the preciseness of thought that cramped space offered. Grabbing her notebook and blanket, she settles onto the carpeted floor of the thin closet. Sterile and empty, the metal doors do not insulate like the wooden door of her childhood cocoon.

Yet she remains, remembering the good fortune of freedom. Just as in her childhood closet, she cradles her notebook in her lap and starts a list. Lists of ten fill the pages of her life. Any dilemma can be drawn to its narrowest points with ten questions.

1. How old were the Senton women?
2. Why did they leave the club?
3. What does Robert's mother know?
4. Who wrote the note?
5. What is Pearce Cotton?
6. Who is my father?
7. Who is buried in the first city?
8. Is the bell important?
9. What is the ninth key?
10. Why did I end up in NY?

Now, the hard part. She must answer each question with a truth, no matter how brutal. Lara buried the childhood lists

96

among the leaves of her wooded back yard. Tonight's answers are less concrete, but still hold danger in their revelation.

1. No idea
2. No idea
3. We will have to meet.
4. Hunch - her mother
5. No idea
6. No idea
7. No idea
8. Yes, it is on the medallion.
9. No idea
10. No idea

All hunches. Exiting the closet, she grabs the condensed encyclopedia she bought for college. There has to be something in here about a ninth key. She searches on 9th and ninth.

Nothing except *Beethoven's 9th*, Ninth Key restaurant, and Ninth key of the Mason. She notes the Mason's key. Could it be something? There's an old Mason Hall at the center of the Cotton Exchange building.

The phone rings. *Probably Mom again. Such a worrywart.*

"Goodnight, Lara," Robert's voice is low and seductive.

His timing is impeccable. She is ready to close the book on this long, interesting day, and coos her own goodnight wishes, settling into the bed they shared just hours before.

"Goodnight, Robert, I'll call you tomorrow."

Chapter 19

June 13, 1991

Drumbeats end another dream family march, and Lara hits the snooze button, knocking the alarm clock to the floor. The sound persists. It's the phone.

"Hello."

"Miss Bonavito, this is the front desk. We have a delivery for you. May we send it up?"

"Nah, I'll come down. Give me a few minutes." She throws on sweatpants and a white tee, excited to see what it is. Waking energized and blissfully bulletproof, Lara doesn't care what the lobby dwellers will think of her sloppy outfit.

Robert's attention has transformed her. Sharing such intimacy gives a temporary reprieve from the unbearable burden of insecurity, but how long will it last?

"Get out of town," she blurts when she sees Abel leaning against the concierge stand. He hands her a basket filled with chocolates, cookies, and fruit.

"Well, that ain't the usual response." Abel tilts his salt and pepper beret in greeting. "Seems you and Mr. Robert getting on okay. Unless this is his way of makin' up for something devilish."

"Not devilish. At least I hope not. Let's talk." Lara points to the same lobby seating where Robert surprised her yesterday.

Lara places the heavy basket on the glass coffee table and they sit across from each other.

"My medallion is real." The statement comes out like a prizewinning proclamation. She gets the guy and a connection to Savannah.

"You sure?"

"Pretty sure."

"You find what you looking for in Savannah then?" Abel grins.

"Well, kind of. But you might be able to help clear something up."

"Never know. I'll sure try."

Lara explains, "At home, I found a note that made me think my family's from this area, and it mentions a cotton race. My marker in the Chamber lobby says Pearce Cotton. Ever heard of it?"

Abel looks down at his pointy cowboy boots, trying to remember. "Miss Lara, I know I heard that name." The lines around Abel's eyes deepen as he accesses the memory.

"I recall somethin' 'bout a Pearce killed at the old Episcopal Church down Bull Street. That place burned down. If this old head is on straight this morning, was just after the war.

"Course, could be a ghost story. Tour guides make up all kinda stuff." Abel's grin widens, and Lara ignores the obvious Robert dig.

"Story goes, he died at the altar. Have to be pretty mean to kill a praying man. I think that Pearce had some sorta business in west Georgia."

Abel's eyes widen as another detail surfaces. "If I ain't mixin' memories, that Pearce did something good before he died. 'Cause hundreds of black folks lined the street for his funeral. Drove him past the Cotton Exchange, even rang the city bell for him.

"Get out of here."

"Well, Ms. Lara, that's twice you kicked me out."

"Sorry, no, I mean, there's a bell on the marker that Robert showed me. Has to be him. Newspaper probably covered it. Do you know where he's buried?" Lara asks. Her list of possibilities is growing at an impossible rate.

"No idea. I best get back to the shop. Robert might have ordered a few more of these." Abel chuckles at his own joke.

"He has not." Lara swats Abel's shoulder playfully, hoping he's wrong.

She nibbles at her cheek, quelling the urge to ask Abel how many times Robert has sent romantic gifts through his shop.

Abel leaves, and Lara reads the card. "Hope you're on the mend. See you soon. Robert Taylor."

She will call Robert, then Susan. Susan's perspective will be a much-needed respite from the questionable motives of all the male conversations.

Robert answers on the second ring, thrilled to hear from her, and invites her to dinner at the Pink House. In tour mode, he describes the pink stucco of the restaurant's exterior, explaining that the building was originally built for a cotton factor named James Habersham, Jr. Robert adds a touch of touristy intrigue, "Haunted, too, by a man who hanged himself in the basement."

Lara accepts, and as she hangs up, the phone rings again.

"Lara, it's Susan. What ya doin' girl? I'm telling you, your story is more excitin' than snuff. I didn't sleep a wink. Get ready. We're going to the historical society. Only members get to peek at the juiciest gems in that paper tomb, and I'm bustin' you in. Hope you don't mind me tromping along."

"Mind? I can't wait," Lara says. "I need a woman to run some stuff by. Too much testosterone around of late, if you know what I mean."

"Honey, there's never enough testosterone. How 'bout I meet you down there. It's at Hodgson Hall, down on Whitaker, near the park. Need directions?"

"Nah, I'll get them from the front desk. Susan, your accent doesn't sound like other Savannahians. Where are you from?"

"L.A."

"Really? You sound southern."

"I am. That's Lower Alabama."

Susan laughs so loud that Lara has to take the phone from her ear. "Okay, L.A., I'm gonna shower and get ready for the paper tomb."

Chapter 20

June 13, 1991

Hodgson Hall is next to Forsyth Park, one of the first places Lara sought out in Savannah. At the time, the park fountain seemed the quintessential representation of the city.

Now, as she drives past the cascading water and spouting swans, she believes the historic buildings of Savannah are its true heartbeat. Restoration is the spine of Savannah's survival. Without the resurrected buildings, Savannah tourism numbers would plummet.

Hodgson Hall, built in 1875, looks like someone picked it up off a Greek island and plopped it down on Whitaker Street. Huge pillars flank the double doors, and the exterior is a spackled tan. The guide map describes it as a "Mediterranean marvel."

A laundry list of no-no's and documents greet her entry. The research application asks for her research intentions, driver's license number, and home address. Lara turns over her pens, backpack, water bottle, and umbrella for safe storage.

Carrying only a notepad and pencil, Lara heads to her assigned table. Solid oak and large enough to accommodate a Bonavito family reunion, the table flanks oak bookshelves brimming with reference material and binders. The shelves continue behind a protective iron railing on the second level.

A painting of William Brown Hodgson stands like a soldier at the end of the room. Hodgson's expression looks like he'd rather be anywhere on earth than posing for the artist. An oriental rug at his feet and a paper-laden desk add authority to his seemingly annoyed stance.

Lara requests information on anything related to Pearce Cotton and the attendant explains, "Our collection houses documents and artifacts, stored by subject and indexed in the binders you see there."

With the attendant's help, Lara locates the binder she needs. Seeing the words "Pearce Cotton" in print moistens her palms and quickens her heart. They are just two of the millions of words stored in this repository of Georgia's roots, miniscule in the scope of the collection, yet powerful enough to reassure and terrify.

As Lara notes the collection name and the file numbers on the card, she pictures Pandora, and how once she opened the box, she could never escape what she found.

The material she requests covers 1892 to 1938, and its contents include a general ledger, financial documents, and correspondence for a Pearce Cotton Mill in Muscogee County, Georgia.

Lara hands the card in at the front desk, and the attendant heads off to locate the collection saying, "I'll deliver it to your table in a few minutes."

Susan arrives in a flourish of flowing fabric, oversized sunglasses, and complaints at the indignity of turning over her gold pen at the front desk. "Darling, if I told you what I did for that pen, you'd be redder than the drapery."

Just as the archivist is about to reply, a scholarly looking man complete with bowtie and traditional goatee taps Susan's shoulder and gives her a welcoming hug. Susan waves Lara over, and after a brief introduction, Major, as he calls himself, shows them to the back of the venue. "This section houses an original draft of the US Constitution, so you understand the importance of keeping it under lock and key."

The informal tour continues, and Lara pays careful attention when the Major mentions genealogical records. They might have a death record for the Pearce murdered at the church. Lara looks back at her table in the main research room where a box now waits.

After their gracious host departs with strict instructions to contact him should they need additional assistance, Susan suggests they chat for a minute before divin' into the dust.

Lara and Susan leave the echoing walls of the immense reading room and head outside. The hustle and bustle of street noise is a welcome departure from the hushed interior. Leaning against the scrolled and pointed black iron railing of the front stoop, Susan asks about Robert.

"He your beau?"

"Well, sort of. I like him a lot."

"Girl, who wouldn't? He's handsome, nice dresser, soft-spoken. If he has money, get yourself hitched."

Lara laughs, wishing things were as straightforward as Susan sees them.

"He's been great, helped me tie together some search strings, but he's got strings of his own. Seems Robert's had one-nighters with quite a few tourists. He's a trolley guide; does it to quell boredom. The job, I mean, not the one-night stands."

They both smile.

"I think we hit it off because he's so interested in history. His mom is a bigwig in a few restoration groups. She's probably a member here, too."

"Boredom and history, a perfect pair." Susan grins again.

Lara frowns, thinking that boredom is also what led Robert to the women. *How long before he's bored of me?*

As if reading her mind, Susan chimes in, "My lord, child. So, he's met a few young ladies. Just look at him. He obviously believes the sun comes up just to hear him crow. With that kind of crowing, it's no surprise women take to him like flies on honey. No sin in that."

"Yeah, but he's used some creepy tactics to reel them in."

"For instance?" Susan raises a well-shaped eyebrow, obviously intrigued.

"Well, there's a wall of historical markers at the Chamber of Commerce on Bay Street. Have you seen them?" Susan shakes her head.

Even as she explains it, Lara has trouble picturing Robert in the act and can't understand why a rich, good-looking man would bother to calculate such deceit.

A police officer passes on horseback. "Pheeewww-wooo," Susan lets out a catcall. The officer tilts his hat and continues towards the fountain.

"I can't wait to hear what you think about this." Lara sits on the top step. Susan joins her. "Robert's been changing up some of the historical markers at the Chamber to create some sort of bond with the women. I guess he's an artist.

"He finds out why they are in Savannah and makes a personal marker for them. The kicker is, he doesn't just give the art to the women; he hangs them in the lobby and acts like they've been there forever.

"He had one for me. Of course, I never questioned his motives. I mean who makes up history to get laid? But, my marker was real."

"So instead of one-liners, this good ol' boy concocts a bit of history. Can't shoot a guy for trying. And he told you the truth?" Susan flaps a hand, as if brushing away Lara's concern.

"Yes, but..."

"No buts about it, Lara. If ya don't mind me saying, God works in mysterious ways. You've been searching for somethin' and he sent ya a man with a medallion. Just ride that horse till it drops."

Lara imagines the ride and smiles, hoping that Susan is right. Not questioning his motives is easier and more fun than dwelling on it.

"Now, about your mama, tell me what you know."

Lara explains the clues included in the letter and the array of family possibilities she's considering.

Susan hangs on every word and when Lara is done says, "Well, if the dead Pearce from the church is a clue, he's likely a relative of your mama's. If she wrote the letter, she wanted ya to know 'bout him for a reason."

"That waving gal also sounds important, but without a Pearce in the flapping family, the Senton women might be your best bet. Get that artist of yours to set up a meeting with his mother. It's time to pick the old bird's historical brain. Now, what're we getting all sneezy 'bout in there?" Susan gestures to the door.

"I'm looking for the Pearce from the church or something about Pearce Cotton. Anything that ties it all together. I already asked them to pull a box on the Pearce Mill."

"Well tie me to an anthill and fill my ears with jam, what are we doing out here then?" Susan is at the door, holding it open for Lara.

Lara laughs at the image as they head back inside. Susan pokes around the public collection, leaving Lara to her box. The cardboard container is next to her pad and pencil. Hands shaking, Lara pries it open and refers to the list of contents. The first document she takes from the folder is a work order dated 1890, with an attached land grant made out to Samuel Pearce, Jr. The grant is for twenty-seven acres in an area "above and beyond the confines and limits of Columbus City." The paper is stamped with an official-looking wax seal that reads "Muscogee County."

Samuel Pearce could be the man from the church.

The mill's financial records are in folder seven and show that the textile mill opened in 1892. There is a thin ledger filled with documents, numbers, and words which make little sense to Lara. She skips these pages whose ancient curly cues and handwriting are undecipherable.

Despite not being able to read it all, Lara savors each paper. The handwriting and smell of the antique parchment remind her of the distance she has travelled to uncover her mysteries. Like heirlooms from an attic, each page reveals something forgotten that could hold untold value.

Flipping ever so gently through the pages, she reads the names and meager wages of the mill workers. Mill positions listed next to each name include Doffer, Opener, Picker Hand, Card Hand, Spooler, Twister, Warper, Band Boy, and Sweeper. Two years of wages appear, followed by a blank page, with a simple note in a different handwriting. "Samuel Pearce, RIP. 1894."

The next folder includes the ledger for 1895 through 1936. Inside the cover is a list of three mill owners, all Pearce's: Samuel Pearce II, Benjamin Pearce, and Thomas S. Pearce. The ledger ends with Thomas. *My grandfather?* she wonders.

Susan sits at the other end of the table with her own historical goodies, a box of the most recent jail records she could find for Georgia moonshiners. Seeing that Lara has closed her box, Susan slides closer. "Girl, I'm hunting down a new husband. These fools got moonshine AND money. How can I go wrong?"

"Look at this, Susan. I found the Pearce names from the mill. All of the owners were Pearces. Paper trail ends in the thirties."

Ecstatic to have found Pearces from the cotton industry, yet unsure of what to look at next, Lara suggests they finish up.

Like a lightning bug freed from a mason jar, Susan nearly flies down the outside stairs singing, "Found me a man, drunk as can beeee. Don't care if he's living, just want his moneeee."

They giggle all the way to Lara's car. Lara hugs Susan and assures her that she will call. Susan is off to an appointment on Barnard Street. "Some old butcher's house. Maybe I'll get me some meat."

"Ugh, you're so bad."

107

Susan shouts as Lara drives by, "Bad is good, honey child. Keep telling ya self that."

Chapter 21

June 13, 1991

Back at the hotel, Lara opens the Chatham County phonebook to the page with the three Pearce listings crossed off. On the hunt for a modern day ancestor to Samuel, Benjamin, or Thomas Pearce, Lara hopes to find at least one name that matches the mill ledger.

Below the Senton numbers in her notebook, she writes the number of the only Thomas listed. The Senton calls can wait until she finds out what Robert's mother knows about the women who resigned from the Altrusa Club.

At the desk, designed with the business traveler in mind, Lara lifts the phone and puts it back, unsure what to say. Every option that comes to mind is ludicrous. She can't just ask some stranger if they lost a kid. She needs a script.

She dials 9 for an outside line, then 651, and hangs up again. Her hand is shaking. Remembering the bottle of rum she'd stashed in her suitcase for the trip, she downs a shot of liquid courage and dials the entire number.

"Hello." His drawl is no surprise, but reminds Lara that she is a stranger. Reminding herself to take it slow and listen, she begins.

"Hello, my name is Lara Bonavito. I'm looking for Thomas Pearce."

"This is he."

"Um, I'm doing some genealogy research, looking for a Thomas Pearce whose family managed a cotton mill in the 1930s."

"Ah, that'd be my father. He moved to Charleston years ago. Not selling anything, are you?"

"No sir." Lara uses the Southern term of respect, to assure the stranger of her trustworthiness.

"Sir, may I ask what your mother's name is?"

"Mom passed in eighty. Her name was Marianne. Is that who you're looking for?"

Lara responds, "Uh, well it might be."

Thomas continues, "Marianne was a Senton though. She kept her maiden name, so she was technically a Pearce, but never in public."

Senton is the name of the women from the Altrusa Club. Lara stares at the Senton phone numbers in front of her. Standing now to steady herself against the hotel wall, Lara continues.

"I know these questions are a little personal…but do you have a sister?"

"Virginia. She's gone too."

Lara drops the phone. Up, up, up her hopes have traveled, and then the ride is complete, a hard landing. Virginia might be her mother, and she's dead. Praying he means that she is gone from Savannah, Lara breathes more slowly, in order to retain her composure.

Lara picks up the phone, focused on keeping Mr. Pearce on the line. Despite the churn of emotions that accompany her first conversation with the man she believes to be her blood uncle, she has to get as much information as possible, in case this is their only conversation.

"I believe we're related," she says, her voice shaky. She speaks the words in a trancelike state. The drums of the dream family start in her head and fade again. Lara questions if they are saying goodbye.

"Can we meet? I'm here from New York to, um, research my roots. Do you have time this week?"

"Sure," Thomas seems curious. "Hang on, let me look at my calendar." There is silence on the line as Thomas gets his calendar. Lara holds the phone to her ear, taking slow, deep breaths. "Why don't we meet at my home? I'm on West Perry. Thursday evening okay? Tomorrow is rather tight."

"Yes, that's fine."

Writing down the address, Lara repeats it. This could be the most important address Lara has ever known. West Perry Street may be her place of final, blessed found-ness.

"Thank you, sir." Lara hangs up and weeps with relief and disbelief. If she is correct, and the clues are true, she will meet her blood uncle day after tomorrow. At last, she will have her own flesh and blood someone, a kind, educated relative who is truly hers.

Picturing him, sitting in front of her with the same green eyes and nose she has examined in the mirror for all of her life, Lara worries about his acceptance and the accuracy of her familial deductions. It has to be him. The Sentons are Pearces, and they were members of the club that commissioned the statue.

Lara thinks of all the questions that have defined her life. Answers are her fairy tales, so far removed from reality that the idea of them is hazy and unfathomable.

As her chest muscles loosen and the sobs retreat, Lara hears the words again. "Virginia is gone too."

The smoky façade of her resemblance to Thomas Pearce fades and the dark possibility of never knowing gnaws at her. Elation exits under the finality of the words. If Virginia is her birth mother, her dreams of reunion could be over.

Sobbing overtakes her again, and Lara cries until the world returns to its previous wash of painful unknowns. In order to survive the tumult of emotions surrounding the call, she pushes the truth to the precipice of reality. It's safe there, at least until she meets Thomas Pearce.

Chapter 22

June 13, 1991

Lara dresses in her only black dress, a strapless sheath she's worn for every wedding, birthday, and social occasion in her adult life. Packed with the hopes of wearing it to meet her birth mother, the dress's loveliness has dulled with the predicted mourning.

Her birth mother is probably dead. "Find something positive, Lara." Her mother's advice surfaces, a reminder of home. No matter what she finds, she has options. No sense dwelling on it until she confirms the facts. Lara straightens her shoulders, dabs on more powder to cover the cry craters under her eyes, and heads to the lobby to meet Robert.

He is dressed in a perfectly fitted gray suit and holds a white rose. He looks at her in a way that both warms and warns. In college, it was this kind of look—enticing and protective—and the tentative magic of physical exploration that sustained and unraveled her. She aches to be sheltered and loved. Looking at Robert, she wants to hold onto this feeling forever.

The dinner date is a perfect combination of romance and friendship, yet anxiety continues to scratch at her innards. The more she shares of her search, the closer she feels to Robert. Yet, the dishonesty of the damned historical markers nags her to stop, yield, go back, and ask.

With its warm breeze, soft music, splendid food, and sweet innuendos, this would be a perfect night to surrender. Lara traces Robert's hand with her finger and looks into his eyes, deciding if she should just accept his lies as the past. Susan thought it was okay.

After eating the best peach cobbler she has ever tasted, the question slithers closer to the tip of her tongue. Sweetness and dread mingle there until it erupts.

"Robert, I have to ask you about the bank markers."

"Yes?" his fork scrapes the plate, imitating a nails-on-chalkboard squeal.

"I met someone, actually he sought me out the night after you showed me the markers at the bank. He said..." Lara lifts the crystal goblet and gulps down its contents. "Well, he said you put up fake medallions in the lobby to seduce tourists."

Freeing the words is a relief. Lara's shoulders relax and she waits for his answer.

"It's true."

Oh God, Lara's shoulders fall. Her hope deflated.

"It's true, but not how you think." Robert is talking too fast. "I told you I spent a lot of time in that lobby as a kid waiting for my parents. I had a lot of idle time and I found ways to fill it."

She lowers her eyes to the napkin in her lap.

"I'm not making excuses, Lara."

"Go on," she says, no longer sure she wants the truth.

"Who told you?" Robert asks her.

"Rather not say."

"Look, Lara, I've been sculpting the markers as gifts for years. The first one was of old Union Station. My father used to talk about the last train that went through there. So, I sketched it and molded the scene in clay on a leftover disc from one of mother's restorations. I made the medallions into Savannah scenes and gave them as gifts to my family."

He smiles, in an effort to lighten the mood.

"I told my parents about the markers when I was a kid, but they didn't want to hear it. When I was eight, we saw something on television about the Davenport House. I tried to tell my mother about the Davenport marker, and she told me to stop going on about the bank and things that I had no connection to.

"I never forgot it. I waited at the bank after school every day and grew to love the markers. When mother insisted that it had nothing to do with me, it hurt."

Lara imagines Robert as a boy in the bank lobby. She imagines a school uniform and his youthful silhouette beneath the three-story, metal-barred windows.

"I didn't use them to seduce anyone. I met a woman on my tour and she told me about a relative who died at Fort Pulaski. It meant so much to her, so I made a disc of the fort. She met me at the bank, because it felt odd just handing the thing to her so I put it on the wall. I wanted her to find the connection and she loved it," Robert defends. "She'll tell her kids someday, Lara, and they'll feel the same bond to Savannah. I make the medallions to keep Savannah alive."

"Yeah, in a really screwed up way," Lara whispers.

Robert does not seem to hear her. He wrings his hands guiltily. "It was not about sex. I promise. It's about Savannah."

Lara contemplates Robert's insecurity.

"Really, Lara. I'm not kidding. When you mentioned Pearce and the cotton clues, I damn near lost it. I knew those words were in the lobby. When I took you there, I thought of all the times I created connections and how this time, you gave me one. Somehow, I had a piece of what you needed to find your family. It's insane."

"Yes, it is, but I think I get it," Lara speaks the words to the floor. Every word Robert is saying mirrors her mixed up mindset.

"Seems like everyone is searching for something, Robert," Lara watches his face relax. She has let him off the hook.

"I was, I am, but this could be something real, Lara. I know it."

How can she fault him for giving away the same bond that she's been searching for her entire life? Unlike the others, her medallion was real and that solidifies their connection somehow. Lara's internal warning system activates, and she kills it like a cockroach.

"I am glad you know," Robert sounds relieved. "Let's get out of here."

Lara sits close to him in the car, thinking about the parental inadequacies that bond them. Is a connection based on childhood need healthy? Too bad. She needs him right now. Relief and warnings compete for her attention. Letting him off easy is simpler than looking closer. With her head on his shoulder, uncertainty dissipates as shared secrets and empty places unleash their seductive power.

Street lamps seem to cast a celebratory dance on sidewalks as they drive through the city. Robert lives in a narrow row house, hugged on both sides by identical dwellings. Long narrow steps lead to the first floor, and a much shorter flight brings them to his expansive bedroom. An ancient, four-poster bed stands before the immense fireplace. Dark wood floors let out a creak as he lifts her onto the bed.

He lies next to her. They are still. The intimacy shared in long stares, only arms touching, is nearly as intense as the lovemaking that follows. Its own entity, the needy connection that joined them, lies there too, and its presence frees Lara from self-scolding and suspicion.

When Robert finally kisses her, the release liberates her from the pained shadow of childhood. Something blooms and breaks free. Cobwebs of fear fall away, and Lara allows Robert's touch to overtake her.

Lara rides the wave of his caring, finally allowing fulfillment beyond the physical. His heaviness against her bare skin is no longer a hiding place for the frightened little girl in the closet. Exposed by choice, each crest of physical pleasure delivers a new sense of adulthood and independence.

Staring at the ornate cornices on the ceiling, Lara is suspended between a calm bay of what has been and a vast ocean of what is becoming her new truth. The faces of the family she's dreamt of for years are now cast with real names. They are Thomas and Samuel Pearce, and they owned a real mill.

No longer do they float before her distorted and featureless. Tonight, lying in Robert's bed with its ancient posts and lush linens, she is authentic. The disclosure of previously unknown details has made her feel more concrete. She imagines the feeling is common for most people, yet marvels at the strangeness of knowing who she is.

Revelation has repercussions. Lara remembers her mother. The purposeful resuscitation of records sealed in a vault at the Child's Aid Foundation could kill her. Lara knows that once revealed, the truth would shatter her mother's fragile self-importance. It will take every fiber of Lara's bravery to reveal the secrets Savannah has held for nearly twenty-one years.

Robert's exhalation against Lara's bare shoulder is proof that the past is not content to remain buried. His life is a revelation of hers. His childhood menagerie of medallions held her history. What he embellished in lonely exile bore a truth that would ultimately set her free. Unavoidably, history claws its way out of the dust because it can never really die. As alive and energetic as the lives that form it, whether tortured or treasured, it demands to be inherited.

As memories fall into new categories of before and after Savannah, Lara contemplates the arranged identity she inherited. She pictures her mother's joyful eyes as she revealed the color television she'd saved a year to buy and counters the memory with her ragged voice upon learning about the search.

No matter how much Maureen loves Lara, the missing mother lurks in the shadows, a thorny reminder of the truth. Lara knows that her mother's survival depends on the fanning of the fantasy. Her role as mother is all that is left. No longer a wife or daughter, Maureen embraces Lara with a made-up history in order to survive. It is too painful to contemplate what will become of her now.

Robert mutters in his sleep, and Lara considers how her search might help him past his loneliness. Robert is proof that money really can't buy everything. He works a job he doesn't need and plays games to connect with anyone who looks his way. It's all a bit nuts.

Admiring the masculine mahogany dresser and opulence of the room, Lara imagines her return to the New York apartment with its banged-up, hand-me-down furniture and projected roles. Despite her rebirth, the old life waits unaffected.

Lara's life before Savannah is a black and white re-run, while the revelations of the past few days are new and shine in rainbow hues so vibrant she fears they'll wash away the graying images of before. She can feel the amalgamation of her identities beginning and knows that an agreement will be necessary to survive the churn.

Hours ago, she agreed to believe Robert. Upon finding the letter, she agreed to move through the tumult of searching, no matter the cost. Agreeing to move forward was easier than finding. Setting aside what has always been true to make room for new truths is the most agonizing agreement yet.

Searching has been difficult, but finding may destroy every reality she's ever known.

Chapter 23

June 14, 1991

Retreating as quietly as possible and leaving the door open just enough to watch Lara sleep, Robert calls his mother from the sitting area just outside his bedroom. Lara's face is serene. Gone is the dogged determination of the searching girl on the trolley. Robert hopes that a meeting with his mother will reveal facts that transfer the same tranquility to Lara's wakeful features.

"Yes, Mother, a meeting today if possible. You may have information that could help my friend, Lara. I remember you talking about the Altrusa Club. Could you look around for anything you have on them? I think she's interested in the Waving Girl period when they were working on the statue."

Barbara Taylor answers in her usual bothered tone, "A tad more notice would have been proper, Robert. I have a meeting at ten at City Hall, and another at three o'clock with the curator at Telfair. Make it noon and bring her here. You can show her the house. I look forward to meeting your young lady."

She continues, and Robert does not bother interrupting, "As for the Altrusa Club, I'll dig around to see if I have anything. We were allies in the same war, fighting different battles. Of course, they took on lesser projects while we were saving those first mansions. I recall some sort of brouhaha around the time they commissioned the Waving Girl statue. I'll see what I can find.

"Robert, will I like this one?" The million-dollar question Robert has been waiting for her to ask.

"I hope so."

"Well, the last one, Robert, she—"

Robert cuts in, "Thanks, Mother. See you around noon."

Robert has introduced his mother to far too many of his female friends, hoping she might find some redeeming quality in at least one. Flaw-finding for Barbara is an Olympic sport in which she proudly holds the gold medal. Once Barbara uncovers imperfection, she weaves it into every conversation until Robert throws up the white flag and ends the relationship.

Once the deficiency is revealed and hammered at unremittingly, Robert cannot look away from it. No matter what a woman means to him or how she has pleased him, his mother's overbearing jealousy unsettles his certainty.

Reflecting on how effortlessly his mother usurps his opinion and plays with his affections, Robert hopes that this time he will succeed in ignoring whatever faults Barbara casts on Lara.

Barbara Taylor believes that she owns the men in her life, but she does not possess the emotional tools necessary to nurture them. She keeps Robert close enough to squash, yet far enough away to avoid facing her own failures as a parent.

Robert will not lend even an ounce of concern to what his mother says this time. He prepares for her onslaught of clawing observations by making a mental list of the faults she will find in Lara. She's from the North. She does not know her lineage. She is bold and outspoken. She's traveling alone, scandalous in his mother's eyes. Her parents are divorced. Her clothing is not from Fine's department store, the only place a truly reputable woman would shop.

All of it will be fodder for his mother's faultfinding wrath. Robert does not look forward to the attack but will weather it in hope of helping Lara find background on the statue. The only other option would be to avoid the character-cooking altogether. Robert only agreed to bring Lara to the inquisitor's den because of the information grasped in his mother's perfectly manicured talons.

Lara needs to know who her family is, and Robert wants to help her find a waking calm as beautiful as the one that now permeates her sleep.

Chapter 24

June 14, 1991

Stepping into Robert's childhood home is like venturing onto the Titanic, with women clad in glistening gowns and men in top hats mingling before a feast at china-laden tables. This is what Lara imagines when she pictures Savannah's early days, when cotton was king, and slavery was the backbone of a white man's success. She doubts that Robert thought of the builder's forced contributions even once while playing in the swanky confines of his childhood home.

The thought would never have crossed Lara's mind before talking to Abel about the Pearce killed at the church and all of the black men and women who attended his funeral. Even without knowing whether the murdered Pearce is her relative, Savannah is painted a darker hue. Robert and the bloodline she is unveiling have transformed her from admiring tourist to involved observer.

Robert's parents live on East Gaston Street, a busy road lined with graceful oaks and moneyed occupants. Although smaller than its grand neighbors, the home impresses with high ceilings and a welcoming aroma of oil-rubbed antiques and freesia. Lara feels woefully underdressed in her jeans.

Robert takes her to a formal seating area he calls "the parlor." Four carved mahogany chairs with elaborate upholstery surround a round table set with a silver teapot, china teacups, saucers, dessert plates, linen napkins, and tiny spoons.

Organized with nary a crumb out of place, a tray of tastefully arranged teacakes creates a three-tier centerpiece.

Robert's mother enters the house in a hurry, dropping a pile of envelopes on a granite-topped table by the front door. The woman's confident and stylish entrance intimidates Lara. Barbara wears a flattering yellow suit with padded shoulders, a perfectly fitted skirt and matching pumps. Lara sits taller in the straight-backed chair.

"Robert, are you here?" his mother croons into the echoing cavern of rooms.

"Here, mother," Robert answers, and Lara watches her spin on one yellow heel to face them. Barbara Taylor's initial reaction is neither warm nor welcoming. Instead, the look on her powdered face is curious and disapproving. Lara shifts in the uncomfortable chair, for the dark look in the woman's eyes is unnerving. Robert waves a hand to interrupt his mother's insensitive stare.

"Hello, Mother. Will you join us?" Robert stands to greet Barbara, and following his cue, Lara pops up a bit too quickly.

The look of judgment fades and Barbara responds, "Of course. I'm sorry to be late. Meeting ran over. Let me grab the material I found for you this morning."

Mrs. Taylor's inquisition is as thorough and painful as Robert warned. In typical Barbara Taylor fashion, she announces, "Another tourist, Robert. I'm not sure how you manage these things."

Robert grins and Lara brushes off the first poisonous dart as a joke. However, Barbara's clenched teeth and tight jaw suggest that she is as serious as a Supreme Court judge. Lara shifts in her chair again, waiting for Barbara to address her directly.

"Robert says you're adopted. Where were you born?" she asks, staring at Lara's scuffed black boots.

"New York," Lara answers, tucking her feet as far under the chair as she can manage.

123

"Ah, what does your adoptive father do?" Barbara glances at the oil portrait over the fireplace, nodding to let Lara know the fine looking man is her father.

"I'm not sure. My parents are divorced." Lara can tell from the gold chain dangling from his vest pocket and his confident stare that the man in the painting is wealthy and powerful.

Robert smiles at Lara while savoring a buttery teacake. Wiping the creamy residue from his lips, he announces, "Our Annie is a miracle worker." Annie has been the Taylor family cook since he was a boy. "Mmm," Robert hums his approval, and Barbara shakes her head, probably annoyed that he is eating before pouring a single cup of tea.

"Did your family accompany you to Savannah?" Barbara points to the teapot, indicating that Robert should pour.

"No, ma'am. I'm here alone," Lara answers, watching Robert pour the steaming liquid. He hands a cup to each of them.

"I understand you want information on the Altrusa Club. How do you think they fit into your little search?" Barbara pats Robert's knee and sits next to him. Lara watches from across the table.

To calm her nerves, Lara pictures her mother sitting in the empty chair beside her. The specter of a familiar face gives her the courage to speak. When she finally says something, Lara's voice is a timid contrast to Barbara's rigid tone. "Two women left the club in 1970." She looks at Robert as she talks. "Their last name was Senton. The clues that brought me to Savannah mentioned the Waving Girl statue and since the Altrusa Club was in charge of the statue, I'm hoping the women are relatives. They could be my grandmother and birth mother since they left the club around the time I was conceived. I spoke to a Mr. Pearce here in Savannah. The name Pearce is also one of my clues. He confirmed that his mother and sister were members of the club and that his sister traveled North in 1970. So you see, the pieces seem to fit."

"Mmm, hmmm," Barbara says. "Well, when Robert asked about the club, I could not recall much about the ladies who ran it. However, I went through some newspaper clippings I had saved. We preservationists made the paper quite often back then, so I have quite a collection."

With obvious pride, Barbara continues, "We were influential in saving the city's history and reporters ate it up. What looks better on the cover of the newspaper than a before photo of sinfully ravaged real estate and an after photo that puts the Hope Diamond to shame?"

Barbara hesitates for a moment, considering whether or not to help the young woman. Robert has burned through every eligible woman in the city, and while the idea of his marrying an outsider sickens her, Barbara Taylor believes a steady relationship might force him to give up his humiliating position as a tour guide. Barbara decides that anything, even helping the tourist, is worth a try.

Barbara lifts a yellowed newspaper clipping from the table and unfolds it, "I found this, and looking at you now, I think it proves your lineage."

She extends the article across the tea set, and Lara takes it, glancing first at the caption under the newsprint photograph. It reads, "Altrusa Club Commissions Sculptor Felix de Weldon for Florence Martus Statue." Lara begins to read the brief article and stops to glance at the eight women in the photo. In the back row, all the way to the left, she sees her.

Pound, pound, pound. Lara's heart feels like it will topple the teacup resting on the arm of the chair. Her own face smiles back at her from the photo. Thinner, with guarded eyes, but otherwise it is her image. The chin, the straight thin nose, the high cheekbones, they're all there. If someone gave her the image at any other time, she would have tried to recall posing for it. Nothing could have prepared her for the undeniable resemblance.

Robert stands to look at the clipping over Lara's shoulder, and his mouth falls open when he sees the object of her rapt attention.

"Indeed," his mother announces as if lecturing strangers. "The resemblance is uncanny. If that is not your true mother, she's a relative. Perhaps you ARE fortunate enough to have roots in Savannah after all."

Amid the shocked silence, Mrs. Taylor gathers the tea tray, excusing herself to the kitchen.

Robert kneels closer to the photo. The fourth woman in the back row is identified as Virginia Senton.

Lara reads it too and the tears begin. Virginia is her mother. The gloriously familiar features are proof. To see another being with features so personally aligned with hers is stunning. Lara cannot take her eyes from the face, which, while instantly recognizable, is worn by a total stranger.

The man she will meet tomorrow is her blood uncle. She will finally know why Virginia relinquished her. She will also learn whether "gone" means that Virginia is dead or away. Will there be a reunion or will she be found and lost in the same breath? Answers to a lifetime of questions take form on the horizon as Lara holds the first-ever physical confirmation of her identity.

The face in the photograph is hers.

Chapter 25

June 14, 1991

They ride back in silence. Lara looks up only once with an odd half smile as her stomach roars a proclamation of hunger. Robert smiles at her and pats her hand. Lara looks out the passenger window at the strange roads in the strange city, now hers.

A breeze scatters moss across Lara's path as she enters Robert's house again, and she imagines how far the salty whirlwind will travel before it becomes still. When she gets to the kitchen, the aroma of cleaning compounds and the shine of stainless appliances overwhelm her and she sits at the table to avoid falling. She closes her eyes and Virginia-smiles a cloned grin. When she opens her eyes, a sandwich has appeared. Lara takes a bite, looking at Robert from a faraway place.

Robert sits across from Lara, reflecting on his mother's flippant delivery of the news clipping and Lara's dreamlike state since receiving it. It will be curious to see how Thomas Pearce reacts to the news that Lara is his niece. Robert hopes Pearce is not as suspicious and money conscious as his own family. If anyone showed up on his mother's doorstep claiming to be a relative, Barbara would lock down the house and call the police. In Barbara Taylor's world, either you have money or you are a crook trying to steal it.

Thomas Pearce's address assures Robert that they're on equal financial footing, which means Lara's claim may raise red flags. Robert interrupts the quietness. "Lara, the man you're meeting tonight, he's a stranger. I'd feel better if I came with you."

"He's not exactly a stranger, Robert," Lara answers. "He's my uncle. You can drive me, but I want to meet him alone."

Robert is not welcome at the sacred first meeting. When she touches the hand of a blood relative tonight, she will have beaten the ancient, morality-driven adoption system. The system that sealed away her birth records will lose its vice grip on her identity.

Hundreds of mental rehearsals have not prepared Lara for the misery and elation of finding her biological family. With the possibility that the most crucial cast member is gone, the prospect of the meeting is unexpectedly melancholy. Lara will meet her uncle alone, because he is her blood, her lineage, her only connection to the beginning.

The heavens join Lara in her tearful response to the shock. Wind and rain slap at the tall, heavily draped windows. As she moves to Robert's beige couch, the cadence of the rain synchronizes with the pitter-patter of possibilities. Her mind seesaws with the good and bad that is galloping towards her. How will she tell him? At once, afraid and terrified, she imagines how he might react to the resemblance.

In the kitchen, the comforting clang of dishes against cold porcelain tells her that Robert is busy cleaning up. Laying the photo in her lap, Lara closes her eyes and the newly memorized face remains. Her birth mother's face is familiar and easy to comprehend.

Robert's mother allowed her to keep the clipping with a stern reminder that she should photocopy it and return the original as soon as possible. Lara rubs the thin paper between her thumb and pointer finger, caressing the proof of her lineage. The woman who bore her is real and was once photographable. She stood alongside other women, smiling and dreaming, oblivious to the child who would someday cling to the news article and be swept away by her smile.

Numb, yet never more alive or real, Lara feels as if she is moving, thinking and reacting in slow motion. Her limbs and eyes obey, blink, cross, step, but do so as if coated in thick syrup. No longer syncopated, the rain has combined to a single hum. The shutters take up the beat, slapping the house irregularly. Lara looks again at the clipping and more questions bubble up from her sluggish state. Sorrow storms in when she pictures the two women walking away from her birthplace. Virginia had her mother for support, and they were both members of a club that held history dear. What would make them throw away their own blood?

Robert is back, standing in front of her with a hand extended. Lara assesses his physical attractiveness, imagining what his father looks like and if Robert is a look alike.

Furious pounding and a cacophony of water bucketing out of the metal gutters replace the outside hum. Nearby, the sound of a train churns through the storm. "Are the tracks safe for travel?" Lara utters the question, curious whether the train will easily push through storm debris, or stop to let someone clear the tracks. "How close is the train station, Robert?" she asks.

"There's no train," Robert says gently. "Could be a tornado. Lara, we need to move into one of the interior rooms."

The radio warning came while Robert was putting away the silverware. "Please stand by, station KNG will be with you shortly. Conditions in Savannah are favorable for a tornado. A watch has been posted for Chatham and Bryan Counties."

The tornado siren revs up next, accompanied by the chugging roar of what sounds like a speeding locomotive. Robert's house is not close to any tracks.

Concerned but not panicked, Robert moves Lara to the downstairs bedroom. She shuffles as if heavily medicated, her stride floppy and excruciatingly slow. Lara listens, moving wherever Robert leads, oblivious to the danger. The tiny guest room that once served as an under-stair storage closet is the innermost room. Robert takes her there, closing the door to the sound of a massive wind that is now causing the lights to flicker.

Her inability to focus becomes even more apparent as she turns to him, sets the newspaper clipping on the bedside stand, and begins to unbutton his shirt. His panic turns to arousal and there is no tension in her body as she draws him to her. His senses at full alert, the danger of the storm intermingles with physical pleasure, and the dance ends with sleep.

He wakes in impenetrable darkness and thick quiet. Feeling for his pants, he trips twice before pulling them on. Robert runs his hand along the rough wall, trying to locate the shelf at the back of the tiny hideaway. Feeling around for a flashlight, he shakes a palm-sized, rectangular box, and is relieved to hear the loose rattle of matchsticks. Striking one, he takes a yellowed candle from the shelf and lights it.

He turns back to the bed. She's gone. The newspaper clipping Lara placed on the side table is also gone. Panicked that she may have gone out in the storm, he opens the slanted door. A breeze greets him. The front door is open and he can make out a silhouette on the dark porch.

The candle flickers causing the wax to drip onto his thumb. He snuffs it out, joining her outside. A large limb of his favorite twenty-five-foot magnolia, dozens of palm fronds, and a mass of gray moss litter the street. The welcome luminosity of a full moon peers down from the cloudless sky. Electricity is out for as far as he can see.

Lara is not looking at the debris or the moon. Instead, her eyes stare at the space where two green steeples welcomed her the day before. Vanished is the top of one beautiful tower along with its gilded cross.

Robert surveys the damage in awe. "I'll be damned, a tornado touching down in the historic district. There's a first time for everything." Robert stands behind Lara, wrapping his arms around her waist. She is shivering under a thin, blue blanket. They listen to the sirens and watch as the frantic red and white lights of emergency vehicles illuminate Lafayette Square.

Lara jerks away from him, suddenly distraught. "I missed my meeting with Thomas Pearce. I didn't call, he was waiting for me. The storm...oh, God, he'll think it's a scam."

She looks at the empty spot atop St. John's Cathedral and prays that the tornado is not a sign of things to come. She needs the rest of the answers. Only Thomas Pearce can explain how the woman in the photo came to be her mother.

"Oh, Robert, I can't believe I missed it. How could I sleep through the most important meeting of my life? I have to call him and explain!"

She is shaking when Robert leads her back to the open door. "It is the middle of the night," he says. "You'll call him at first light. Power should be back by then. I'm sure he'll understand."

"What if he won't see me now?"

"He will. Come inside. You need sleep."

Lara insists that they return to the stairwell room despite Robert's assurance. "The storm has passed, Lara."

"You never know, Robert. You can never be sure."

Tonight's dream parade is different, as hundreds of ghostly participants march towards her wearing a mask of her exact likeness. "Find her. Find you. Find her. Find you," they chant as they pass through her and disappear.

Chapter 26

June 15, 1991

"Hello," Pearce answers.

"Hello, this is Lara Bonavito. I was supposed to meet you last night. I'm so sorry. We had a storm and lost power. I lost track of time. They think it was a tornado."

"I heard. Didn't lose power here," Thomas replies, a new hesitation in his voice.

The lighthearted tone and curiosity of their first conversation is gone, surely a result of her being a no-show and the time he's had to consider her motives.

"Hang on. I'll look at my calendar again to see if I'm available," he says.

He said "if." Dread ignites a fire and Lara starts to perspire.

There is silence on the line, as she readies herself for rejection.

"How about Sunday? We could meet after church. Say, three o'clock?"

Relieved and tripping over her words, Lara agrees. "Yes, Well. No. I mean, thank you very much. I'll be there this time. I swear."

"What am I supposed to do for two days?" she asks Robert after hanging up. "I will lose it."

"I'll keep you occupied until we meet him," Robert answers, as if talking to a child.

The insinuation of ownership and participation annoys her.

"Robert, I told you that you can drive me, but I want to meet him alone."

Robert nods, though she can see he is unconvinced.

Placing a hand on her hip in defiance, she stares at Robert. It is her search, and the terms of the meeting are hers to set.

"You know, Lara, you might as well check out of the hotel now that you're staying here."

"Uh, no." She blurts it out and he looks surprised.

"I just thought since you're not sleeping there anyway."

To give up the hotel, which she paid for through Sunday would leave no options. Childhood taught Lara the importance of always having an alternative, a clean getaway. Even at public events, Lara makes a habit of finding her seat and circling the venue to find at least two means of exit.

"Not yet, Robert. I already paid for it through Sunday. Maybe I'll check out then. Thank you for letting me stay though."

With power restored, Robert eases her agitated state with the one thing she always finds soothing: food. They share a meal of homemade waffles coated with sweet Vermont syrup from a non-human shaped bottle. For a fleeting second, Lara fears the syrup was a gift from one of the Northern tourist women.

They eat like an old couple, quiet, yet comfortable in each other's space.

"I have to call Susan and tell her about the photo," Lara says.

She can't wait to share the news, hoping that Susan's reaction will help it to seem real. Watching Robert sip his coffee, the unreality of her predicament is altering her perception. Sounds boom and fade and the dining room appears under ice-like fractals. A kaleidoscope of color washes over the scene, matching her capricious mood. The room is stable one moment and ill-defined the next.

Robert has two tours on his schedule for the day. "Have to get ready, beautiful. Want to join me?"

"Getting ready or on the tour?" Lara asks.

"Either," he replies, giving her a kiss on the cheek and heading to the kitchen.

"I'm gonna call Susan. See what her plans are."

"Mhm." The water is running and Robert hums along to a song on the radio that she cannot hear.

"Speak now or forever hawld ya peace," Susan answers.

Lara lays on the thickest drawl she can muster, "How are yaaaaa'aaallllll?"

"That was the worst southern accent I eva' heard, this must be a Yankee. How ya doing, Lara?"

"Well, I have something pretty incredible to show you. I'm at Robert's. Want to meet today?"

"You two having a little sleepover? Yummy. Up for a swim?"

"Uh, I guess so."

From the heavy humidity moistening the tall windows, she can see that last night's storm did little to cool things down. A diversion with the added bonus of a beach breeze and sandy toes intrigues her.

"Tybee Island?" she asks. "Heard them call it Savannah's Beach on TV."

"Nah, better than that. What's Mr. Handsome's address? I'll pick you up at noon."

Robert is shaved and dressed when she meets him on the stairs.

"Well?" He holds her waist, balancing her against the wooden banister.

"We're going to the beach."

"Perfect. I have to run. See you for dinner." As he kisses her goodbye, Lara is struck by the feeling of being outside looking in.

Standing on the elaborate staircase with the entry chandelier glistening over them, she kisses Robert back as if her grasp of his affection is fleeting. She is a poor kid from New York wrapped in the embrace of a wealthy southern man so handsome he melts her insides. The familiar sensation of playing a theatrical role arrives on cue.

He grins and pulls her into him, starting to move her back up the stairs with a knowing grin. Lara nudges him back down. Robert shrugs his shoulders in defeat before blowing her a kiss and heading out the front door.

Chapter 27

June 15, 1991

Susan is wearing a sheer gold cover-up over a black, two-piece bathing suit, dwarfed by an enormous sun hat. Lara has on a one-piece under her clothes and one glance at Susan's barely there belly makes her glad of it. As soon as she gets in the car, Lara opens the window to clear the overwhelming aroma of suntan lotion and Chanel. As they hit the highway, she updates Susan on the news of the last twenty-four hours.

"I think I found my uncle. I'm meeting him on Sunday. I was supposed to meet him last night, but the storm screwed it all up. We lost power and slept in a room under the stairs like hobbits. Did you see the damage to the cathedral?"

Susan hangs on every word and the hour-and-a-half drive seems to pass in an instant.

When they turn down the long wildflower-lined road that leads to the island, Lara searches for baby sea turtles as pictured in the "Turtle Crossing" signs that line the water-flanked road. Counting eight or so bunnies among the daisies and poppies, Lara contemplates their destination.

"Jekyll Island," Susan explains. "It's where all the mucky mucks from up north used to spend their winters. They built a hunting club here and invited the richest, most influential members of society to join. The club stocked the island with a massive number of animals and then shot 'em all. To celebrate, they drank like the dickens in the mansion they called the clubhouse. J.P. Morgan, the Pulitzer's, the Macy's, the

Goodyear's, the Vanderbilt's. Anybody who was anybody had a cottage here.

"Those high falootin' codgers were so rich they bought a new boat every time they got one wet! Their cottages are mansions to us pot pissers. They restored the clubhouse, and I swear, Lara, the food at the Grand Dining Room is better than sex! I'm also partial to Jekyll 'cause it doesn't have any condo clusters or skyscraper hotels."

A sign in the beach parking lot reads "Complimentary Parking for Club Members Only." Susan parks directly in front of the sign, handing a twenty-dollar bill to the skinny teen checking club keys. He handles the placement of their beach chair and umbrella rentals as they unpack the cooler and towels.

Susan is right. Jekyll is an expanse of nearly desolate beach with nary a condo in sight. Even the hotels are built to be unobtrusive. When the tide retreats, she walks with Susan on the newly revealed sand bar.

"This is like a bathtub. My mother would love this," Lara tells Susan, remembering how her mother would stick her little toe in the water at Jones Beach before retreating to the warmth and safety of the beach blanket. Looking down the shoreline at the neat line of matching rental umbrellas, Lara envisions what her mother would think of such opulence.

Back in their rental chairs, Susan applies more SPF 50 lotion and Lara teases her, "It's like watching a contractor spread plaster."

Pulling the wide fuchsia brim of her hat down further over her nose, Susan responds, "Preservation's not just for old buildings. Now, tell me what else you found."

"Well, Robert's mother had a picture of the Altrusa Club and my mother's in it. Want to see?"

"Does a dog lick its butt? Give it here." Lara carefully unfolds the newspaper clipping from the zippered inside pocket of her purse. She shields it from the salty breeze as she hands it to Susan. Susan shakes her head in amazement. "If that ain't your mama, I'm Mother Theresa. You okay?"

Lara puts away the precious paper without looking at it again. "Yeah, I just get kinda woozy every time I see it."

"I can see why. Let's talk about something else then, like how much sleeping you did at your hobbit sleepover."

After lollygagging on the beach for few hours, they rinse off under the cold outdoor shower near the restrooms and head to a late lunch at an outdoor restaurant with an incredible marsh view and a swimming pool out back.

"Dang, that waitress is slower than molasses headed uphill in the sand," Susan says so loudly that the waitress brings drink refills "on the house."

"Susan," Lara shakes her head. "I thought you Southerners were supposed to be polite." The slow service does not dampen the mood, as conversation and laughter are plentiful.

Susan's animated responses and wide-eyed questions lessen Lara's spinning dread of the upcoming meeting with Thomas Pearce. After the meal, they walk around the grounds of the old club, now a five-star hotel, and Lara falls in love with the forties feel and glamour of the place. The lobby and grand dining room boast deeply carved walls, sparkling chandeliers, and the soothing smells of clean linens and savory cooking.

The floors of the immense porch groan with age as Susan and Lara take up residence in two of the dozen wooden rockers that line the painted planks. They rock away the afternoon chatting with a female familiarity that makes the sharing of secrets feel, for the first time in Lara's life, normal. Revelations of who she is becoming make sharing easier, as does the surer footing of tangible Savannah roots.

Susan encourages her quest, keeping the conversation light, carefully avoiding unknowns and joking endlessly. "You are getting real close to the finish line, girl, I'm tickled pinker than a pig at bath time." Susan smiles a giant grin that makes Lara giggle.

"I really am getting close, Susan. Can you believe it?" Susan does not answer, instead resting her hand on Lara's as they watch the ocean inlet pulse in and out with the arriving tide. An occasional splash and joyful holler from the hotel pool intermingles with the sound of their rocking, and row after row of majestic live oaks bow respectfully over their reflection.

"This is my South, Lara," Susan breaks the rhythm, standing to leave. "Soon it'll be yours, too."

Chapter 28

June 15, 1991

L ara returns to the hotel to shower and pack a few things before heading to Robert's. The diversion of the day at Jekyll was perfection. Susan dropped her off at the valet stand with strict instructions to call immediately after the meeting with Thomas.

Her backpack overloaded with clothes and toiletries, she exits through the door closest to the river. Lara can't wait to meet Robert after his last tour and drive home with him. It is desperately hot and she does not take more than ten steps before she is looking forward to her next shower.

Passing the Waving Girl, Lara cannot resist a tiny wave at her Savannah placeholder. Heading down River Street and up to Bay Street, she stops to look at a handmade leather purse in the covered craft pavilion. A quick check of her watch as she turns to head up Factor's Walk reveals that she is early. She stops for a sip of now warm bottled water, sitting at the lion fountain in front of the old Cotton Exchange. Two confused tourists and an executive with his necktie at half-mast cross in front of her, coming from the direction of the Chamber building.

When he comes into view she smiles, delighted to spot Robert's handsome frame. Nearly bounding down the street she is ready to tell Robert about her beach day with Susan. He is moving slowly and she will catch up easily. She stops abruptly when she spots the woman. Robert's arm is around her, sheltering but not quite touching her shoulder. They're heading towards the Chamber. His body language is the same as when he guided her the day they met. Like a tenacious child in a game of freeze tag, Lara remains still as a statue. Hoping he is on an errand, and determined to find out why he is here at five-thirty, when he said his last tour ended at six-fifteen, she dashes across the street about a yard up from the Chamber.

Approaching from the left, she enters the Chamber portico unseen. Hugging the cool marble wall and peering past the receptionist, she opens the door. A security guard eyes her suspiciously, as he passes the vault. The loathsome reason for Robert's rendezvous chills Lara to the core. It has to be the medallions. Desperate to erase the deceptive assumption, she recalls how many times Robert has expressed his love for her. There has to be a reasonable explanation. All she can see is his arm and the predictably pretty, young woman's shoulder.

The long-legged, blonde demon crouches precariously in the corner of the lobby, near the brochures...and medallions. Robert points to one of the damned discs, and as the woman stands, Lara sees Robert's beautiful bicep extend and contract as he places his arm around her slim shoulder.

A hard push of the heavy brass door and she is back in dense air. Lara turns right, hurrying up Bay Street to duck into one of the bustling steak houses. The hostess fumbles with a menu as she greets Lara who waves her away with frantic fanning gestures. The hostess retreats with a puzzled look. Lara peaks out the window, spotting them again despite the tears that now blur her vision. "Oh, my God," she says, putting her hands on her hips, indignant. "He's taking her to Molly's."

Standing in the restaurant foyer, staring at the place where her Robert was supposed to meet her, she sorts through the facts.

Twice, the restaurant pay phone falls from her fingers as she navigates Susan's number. Insane with hurt, she gushes the words between sobs, "He's with another woman. He showed her the lobby. He is taking her to Molly's. Abel told the truth. I am an idiot, Susan."

Susan arrives within ten minutes and Lara gets in the front seat as the blaring honks of outraged drivers try to get around them. The horns are nothing compared to Lara's sorrow. Susan knows the breakdown is about the tour guide or the poor child's kin. Lara cries, and Susan high tails it from the illegal parking spot, up Bay towards the Tybee extension.

Lara calms long enough to say, "It's all a game. I trusted him. What the hell was I thinking?"

Chapter 29

June 16, 1991

Parking two blocks from Thomas Pearce's house on West Perry Street, Lara cannot stall any longer. She has driven past the brick facade and around Chippewa Square three times to kill time and gather enough nerve to stop. The meeting is her first outing from the hotel in a day and a half. Robert called and she ignored him and the seven messages he left with the front desk. Idle and despondent, Lara slept, cried, and ate her way through the realization that he lied.

Patting at her hair and fidgeting with her notebook, she stands on the steps of her uncle's house, looking at the closed drapes and imagining how he will react when he sees her. She raises her trembling finger three times before finally ringing the doorbell. When he opens the door, she smiles at the familiar eyes smiling back at her. Thomas looks at her with more curiosity than recognition. As if suddenly recalling a forgotten fact, he squints slightly before remembering his manners and letting her in.

Striped gold wallpaper sets a bright tone in the room. Gesturing for her to sit, Thomas Pearce explains, "This has been a music room for more than a hundred years. Legions of Pearces have suffered through piano lessons in here."

The furniture is gaudy and enormous. Even the grand piano with its vase of white roses looks minuscule under the chandelier and gilt archways of the room. Lara is too nervous for small talk. "Sir, I'm looking for information on a Pearce family who is related to the cotton industry. I'm adopted. I was raised in New York. The Pearce family I'm looking for could be my biological family."

Thomas is staring at her now, listening and trying to shake the feeling of knowing the young woman. Lara continues, "It sounds crazy, but I came here because I found a letter that suggested Savannah was significant to my birth. You see, sir, I was looking for anything related to a cotton race, Pearce, or the Waving Girl statue."

Thomas listens without interruption, sensing how important the information is to her. All the while, memories of his sister come, and he smiles at the thought of her scolding him when he acted in a manner she considered improper.

Lara keeps talking despite Thomas's faraway smile. He is remembering an occasion when as a teenager he'd arrived home drunk. Outraged, Virginia had thrown him in the shower fully clothed, claiming she wanted to sober him up before he worried their mother to her grave. Virginia was a good sister, and a bit of an old hen.

The girl before him looks like Virginia. Before she had spoken a word, he knew her to be a relative. Lara hands him the note and Thomas recognizes his sister's writing immediately. He cannot stop looking at Lara now. Her eye color and skin tone are dead on. She's a little bit thinner in the lips, with slightly less defined cheekbones, but otherwise, the resemblance to Virginia is uncanny.

Lara watches as Thomas reads the letter.

"Well, the cotton race in your letter is not about cotton, Miss Lara."

"Are you the Pearce in the letter?" Lara shivers at the possibility.

"Not me," Thomas shakes his head. "She meant our great-granddaddy."

Lara is awestruck at Thomas's word choice. OUR granddaddy means that he belongs to her too.

"You said you found the papers from the family cotton mill, so you know the place opened in the late 1800s. My great-granddad, the first Samuel Pearce, built the mill when he was twenty-two, not long after his daddy's plantation failed. The land sold off in small parcels and Samuel used his portion to move up to Muskogee County. Wanted to get as far away from his father as possible. Not proud of it, but there was bad blood there. Truth is the truth though."

Chapter 30

September 16, 1880

The ruckus outside of the schoolroom twisted Miss James' usual smile into a sour smirk. Samuel Pearce tried his best to concentrate and not look out the only window of the tiny wooden classroom. His fellow classmates did not try at all.

Miss James swatted her ruler on the desk. "Emily Marshall, you will continue the passage from your reader, please."

Emily read aloud in front of the class as Miss James walked to the window, looking for the cause of the interruption. Once there, her facial expression shifted from disgust to dismay. Samuel could tell that whatever was happening outside was serious. What started as a murmur grew into a frightening thunder of shouting. Samuel could only make out a few words in the din of men's voices. "Nigga school" and "get 'em out."

Miss James stood mesmerized and Emily, having completed the passage, inched to join her at the window. The rest of the students followed. Samuel was the last to rise from his desk and could barely see past the swarm of bobbing students. The only thing visible to him was a glow of bright light that danced in the distance. The shouting mixed with crying then, and youthful voices joined the chaotic choir. The acrid smell of smoke arrived like a devil sneaking between the wooden rafters, and Samuel worried that the school might be on fire.

Miss James turned from the window at last and said, "Class dismissed."

The announcement was met with applause and curiosity since it was only noon. Miss James instructed, "Go directly home, children."

Outside, the source of the smell was clear. A bright blaze and plumes of smoke rose from the Negro school across the field. Tiny dots scurried through the field in all directions. Samuel could not help but move towards the commotion.

As he approached, Samuel spotted a group of men on horses gathered at the end of the dirt drive to the Negro school. They were a mass of white and did not move to help the children flee from the blazing building which served as both church and schoolhouse. Still as death, the men remained at the end of the drive.

Samuel moved closer, stopping where a Negro woman sat in the weeds, a girl nestled in her arms. The woman prayed aloud. "Lord, help us," she repeated as the child in her arms wailed with a force unrecognizable as human. Charred clothing covered the girl's torso. Her flesh was a mass of bubbled pain. The praying woman looked at Samuel now.

"Help us," she pled, and Samuel was not sure whether she was asking God or him.

"Water. They need water!" Samuel yelled at no one. Bewildered by the men's lack of movement, he moved closer.

"That'll teach them niggas to build a school so close to ours. Samuel knew the voice immediately. Recognition overcame him like a fever. It was his father. He'd burned the girl and her school. Samuel ran as fast as he could toward home, tears flying and his stomach burning with outrage.

Why would his father burn the girl? Why?

Chapter 31

May 10, 1892

At the land auction more than a decade later, twenty-two-year-old Samuel carefully memorized the pained expression on his father's face. Samuel was ready to take what was rightfully his, without remorse. The war destroyed the plantation house, and boll weevils took the crops. Tired and overworked, the land turned back to dust, and the family's fortune was at the mercy of the parcel sale.

Standing next to the broken frame that was once his boyhood hero, Samuel compared his father's distress to the face of the burned child. Gone was the authoritative man on the horse. In his place stood a broken soul, paying the price eleven years later. The sale was brisk, and in the span of ten minutes, all that his father had owned was sold. Samuel pocketed the money from thirty of the sixty parcels sold.

Samuel did not mention the school fire that day nor did his father. Working alongside him for the good of the family, Samuel had waited patiently for the time when God would take away all that his father held dear. Samuel had known his father's devastation would come.

The day after the fire, the students had returned to class with questioning eyes and Miss James made a lesson of the fire, assuring them that, "Goodness is rewarded and evil is punished in God's time."

Now finally, with enough money in his pocket to leave the city of his birth, to depart the dying coast, and build a textile mill near Columbus City, Samuel was ready to go. Looking at his father's bloodshot eyes for the last time, Samuel said one thing before leaving the plantation for good. "It's finally God's time, Daddy. God's time indeed."

Chapter 32

June 16, 1991

"So, Lara, when my great-granddad opened the mill back in the 1890s, he hired more blacks than whites to work it. People called him a unionist. He could have hired blacks to work 'longside whites, as long as he paid them less, but he paid everyone the same and caught hell for it, especially when he visited Savannah. When the white workers went on a three-month strike, it ruined him financially. Blacks were afraid to work, so he was down to half production, a real tough spot. He came to Savannah quite a few times to sell off family heirlooms. Even sold the rocking chair his father carved for his mother when he was born.

"How clever. The Pearced part of this," Thomas holds up the letter. "It's how he died."

"Killed in church?" Lara asks. "Someone I met said there was a Pearce killed in church and that almost everyone at his funeral was black."

"Yes, that was him. My father said they found him on his knees at the altar with a knife in his back. People had no patience for anything but separatism then. After he was killed, my granddad took over the mill, then my dad. I'm on the board now, but we're just shippers these days. Cheaper to process cotton outside Georgia. So that's the cotton race she writes of. Cotton built our family up, and race tore it down, for a while anyway. When were you born?" Thomas is looking at her again.

"December 18, 1970." Lara has been taking notes to keep her emotions under control.

"Judging from the writing on this note, it's from my sister, or someone who knew her writing pretty well. I'm not sure why my sister would have written it, or how you ended up with it. She was a quiet kid, shy actually. You look like her, you know?"

"Thank you, I mean, well, I have something else. There was a photo of Virginia Senton in the newspaper, and it could be...."

Tongue-tied and unsure whether to mention the possibility of his sister being her mother, Lara pushes for confirmation. "On the phone, you mentioned that your sister went north around 1970. Do you know why? I think that might sort things out."

"Well, she went to stay with our aunt in 1970. She was in New York for several months touring prospective colleges.

"Lord, I have not thought of Virginia this much in a long time. I remember when she got back, I teased her mercilessly about her new northern demeanor. She came back so much more outspoken. The trip toughened her up. I remember asking her which college she'd chosen. I can still see her standing there with her hands on her hips, declaring that her feet would never leave Savannah soil again."

"Did she leave Savannah?" Lara asks the question, overwhelmed by the confirmation of Virginia's visit to New York and the reality of speaking to her real uncle.

"No, Virginia lived at home 'til she was twenty-eight. She spent a lot of time in church and in this room playing. She played more games than piano. She'd close that pocket door and lock herself in here playing solitaire or writing for hours. Intrusion was fun. Her anger was extraordinary when I bugged her."

Looking around the room, trying to imagine Virginia in it, Lara asks, "Do you have a photo of her?"

"Sure do." Thomas stands to retrieve the photo from the piano. He looks from the photo to Lara and smiles sadly before handing over the heavy silver frame. "She was around seventeen here."

Startled, she drops the photograph on the Oriental rug below her chair, leaning over to stare at it again. It's all real. Thomas Pearce is her uncle.

Lara remains bent over looking at the photo and Thomas moves to help her. Lara picks up the photo, inspects it for damage, and asks the question she has dreaded. She has to confirm it.

"Where is she now?"

Clearing his throat, Thomas replies, "She was killed by a drunk driver. He was heading the wrong way on Interstate 16. She was just twenty-eight. It was...very difficult."

"Oh, no." Lara is keeping her emotions intact for fear her uncle will escort her to the door or call the authorities. Stabbing the corner of the silver frame hard into her palm, she concentrates on the pain in her hand and not the pulsating pain in her heart. "That must have been so hard on the family."

Lara's mind seesaws, attempting to avoid the clawing pain of the truth. Perhaps the dead woman is not her mother. Maybe her birth mother is a cousin or other relative. That could explain the resemblance. Gnawing and unavoidable are the facts. The handwriting is Virginia's, and the woman in the picture is the same woman from the newspaper clipping. Virginia was in New York in 1970. Lara's reunion picture burns away. All the happy tears, hugs, and examining of familiar strengths melt into blackness.

"Sir," she asks another question, delaying the revelation, hoping to discover that her mother is alive. "I only have one clue left to ask about. Any idea what the ninth key might be?"

"No, I'm sorry I don't." Thomas is trying to figure how this young woman is related. There is no doubt that she's a relative, but how? His sister was shy and awkward with men, and try as he might, Thomas cannot remember her ever dating. Virginia would not have a child and keep it secret. Pearce calculates the timing of the girl's birth. While Lara has not said it, he knows she is looking for her mother. Could it be one of the cousins?

As a kid, he overheard his mother and aunt talking about a cousin who was dropped off stone drunk by two men in a pickup at four a.m. His aunt waited up for her and saw the men toss her there, blouse open, her hair tussled like a rat's nest. Her mother said she was so drunk that she was still tipsy after ten hours of sleep. Cousin Corinne was always embarrassing his aunt.

Thomas decides Corinne could have written the note. It has just enough information for Lara to find the Pearce's, but no details to implicate her. He will investigate further before revealing his hunch to Lara, rather than raise her hopes prematurely.

Pearce stands and says, "I have a museum board meeting at Telfair in thirty minutes. I'd like very much to discuss this further. Are you available to talk again this week?"

"No. I mean yes. I can meet you anytime." Lara is relieved to be parting without the dreaded confirmation. "Please let me know if you remember anything about a key."

Lara leaves the music room, heading back to her car and the darkness of another broken heart. The feeling is all too familiar. The tears are a mix of relief and grief. She knows Virginia is her birth mother. But how could she tell Thomas? The words would not come, as they would force mourning greater than her bruised identity can handle.

Mourning for both the trust of Robert and the loss of her birth mother in one day is too much to consider. A well-dressed couple passes on the sidewalk, and she is removed from the stony truth of the music room conversation. The Robert predicament is a safer place to dwell.

Robert's talk of helping people find the parental connection he lacked made her trust him. Their missing pieces matched, but not precisely. For Robert, a complete set of parents failed to set a path for him to thrive, and no secondary caregiver will ever arrive to rescue the lonely boy from the bank lobby. He has nothing without those medallions.

Driving back to the hotel in a daze, Lara wonders how many of the grown-up looking people around her wear the bruises of parental failure. How many of them make poor choices because of their parents?

Lara walks along the river before heading up to the room. The waves kick up a breeze that quickly dries her tears. Like a magnet to metal, she is pulled back to the Waving Girl. Visits to her statue are the only constant now: solid, still, and unchanging. Florence is like an old friend who accepts her no matter the time of day or reason for her visit.

Lara will not confront Robert. Unlike the family she now holds at arm's length from her broken heart, she will dismiss him without her usual last word. Robert is incapable of connecting, and she no longer needs him to define her significance in Savannah. Deciding to walk away is essential, but the sinewy tangle of blackness around her heart tells her it will hurt forever.

Chapter 33

June 17, 1991

The phone rings at eight a.m., an appreciated rescue from a terrible dream of Robert surrounded by a mass of women, all clawing at his feet as he tosses medallions at them. Lara is surprised to hear Thomas Pearce's voice.

"I'm sorry to call so early." His voice is animated.

"I found your ninth key. It was always here. I can't believe it. I had no idea. I'm so sorry, Lara."

Sitting bolt upright, she is awake. "What do you mean? There's a key in the house?"

"Yes, not a key, Lara. It was in the printer's cabinet on the mantle. I have to show you. Please come this morning."

"I'll be there in an hour."

The house is as she left it. Thomas is unshaven and clearly shaken by what he has uncovered. He looks older. When Thomas hugs her, she stiffens against the sudden intimacy. It is clear that whatever he has discovered has convinced him that they are related. When he releases her, she sees that his eyes are pink from a lack of rest. He looks like he has been crying. Lara cannot imagine what would bring this proper man to tears.

Pearce sits her on the same chaise as the day before and lays a long, wooden box on the table in front of her. She eyes the numbered keys hanging from the handles of each tiny drawer. There are ten.

"It is a printer's box." Thomas is speaking fast. "My grandfather stored his print stamps for the mill in it. As you can see, he also used it to sort keys. My sister and I hid candy in it as kids 'Ninth key hides the candy,' she must have sung it a hundred times. I forgot all about it, until last night."

"These were in the ninth drawer. Honestly, Lara, I have not opened that drawer since we hid candy in it as children." Handing her two papers, Thomas sits. "One is in my sister's hand. The other is from a man I don't know."

Lara opens the thicker letter first, and it is in the same cursive handwriting as her note. It begins:

> If you are reading this, I am not here to meet you, but you have found my family, your family. I secretly named you Aimee, for the French word Aimer, which is love.
>
> I have no idea what you are called now, my child, but in my dreams, you are Aimee. I think of you every minute and am often sure I will go mad with worry. I am writing this in hopes that someday, my sweet Aimee, you will know your truth and understand that I love you despite all that happened to me.
>
> There is no shame in your birth. Stand tall, be brave, and know that you have lived in my heart from the moment you began to grow under it. I pray that you will find solace in your maternal lineage and strength enough to ignore the darkness that I will share here. I want you to live a happy life and pray

you can forgive me for leaving you in
New York.

The four-page letter holds everything Lara hopes to know,
and all that she does not.

Chapter 34

March 3, 1970

"She's just the right age," photographer Harlan Dunbar told Marianne as he looked at Virginia. Marianne noted the nods of agreement among other Altrusa members seated at the meeting table.

"Her likeness and age are a perfect representation of Florence for your statue. Of course, I will be working from photos of Florence. However, Mr. de Weldon also requires photos of a girl her age with the river as a backdrop. As you ladies know, every great artist relies on photographic models," Dunbar continued.

Chatty and energized by a follow-up visit so soon after Mr. de Weldon's visit in January, the women of the club applauded when he finished speaking. The fact that photographer Harlan Dunbar had shown up at the meeting thrilled and surprised everyone except Myrtle Marlin who hoped the minutes for this week's meeting would be a breeze after the exhausting work of deciphering Mr. de Weldon's accent at the last one. During the light applause, Myrtle rubbed her knuckles, thankful for a momentary reprieve.

Dunbar was charming. His cobalt eyes and swept-back hair reminded Marianne Senton of an actor from a movie musical. He was an animated bundle of nerves as he passed around his portfolio, explaining how Mr. de Weldon personally chose him to photograph a suitable model in Savannah. Waving his arm in the direction of the river, he explained, "Mr. de Weldon wishes to capture the essence of Florence with photos of a model at the very river where she waved."

Virginia looked overwhelmed by the attention. Everyone in the room smiled at her. It was an honor to model for such a prestigious sculptor. Despite their enthusiasm, Virginia winced every time the photographer mentioned her physical attributes, and a blush of embarrassment reddened her pale cheeks.

Marianne watched the photographer gesture grandly towards the river and could not help but smile as her daughter's face grew pinker. Virginia's shyness was the reason Marianne brought her to the club. She had hoped it would help her find her voice. The photographer's invitation could be just the thing to peel away some of Virginia's quietude.

Allowing her daughter to work with the photographer might help her shyness but could also wreak havoc with her reputation. Several Savannah families with marriageable young men would write her off if she posed for the photos. Marianne wished there was the option of arranged marriage for her awkward daughter. She does not want her daughter to suffer the same outcast status she faced herself during her dreaded courtship years.

Marianne had refused to attend her Christmas Cotillion, thinking it a silly opportunity for boys to laugh at foolish sixteen-year-old girls parading in white ball gowns. Marianne also preferred pants to skirts and short hair to all those ridiculous up-dos piled up as if reaching for Jesus himself. An endless torment to her parents, Marianne was banned from swimming at ten years old, after being discovered on the marshy inlet behind her parent's home, hanging backwards from the boat with her head underwater. She told her parents she had wanted to analyze the behavior of crabs. How else was she supposed to catch them?

She had caught Thomas Pearce's attention without any such maneuvers. In fact, Marianne did not care about marriage one way or the other. Unlike her friends, she married without any thought of how the marriage might increase her standing on the social catwalk. She married Thomas because he was kind, allowed her to speak her mind, encouraged her to explore, and didn't even blink when she announced on the day of their engagement that she would not take his name. She kept that promise, retaining the surname Senton in honor of her father who insisted that women be judged on what they did and not on how they looked.

As she watched Virginia's shy grin, Marianne was forced to weigh the pros and cons of the opportunity. The publicity would cause Virginia to be noticed by more young men, yet if she were perceived as having career goals related to modeling or acting, the opportunity could do more harm than good. Marianne knew career women could be good wives, but this was Savannah where marriage mattered as much as manners.

As the meeting ended, Mr. Dunbar asked, "Will you allow your lovely daughter to be photographed for the Waving Girl statue, Mrs. Senton? Or perhaps you have a suggestion for alternative models of the same age and elegance?" Virginia looked at her mother, waiting for a response, and Marianne saw that her child was excited.

"Yes, Mr. Dunbar, it will be our honor to allow Virginia to act as the model for the Waving Girl statue. As you know, this is a project the club holds near and dear, and we'd like to thank you for the opportunity to be a part of the artistic process. The club members applauded enthusiastically, and Virginia stood to curtsy at her mother's urging.

Chapter 35

March 5, 1970

Virginia opened the beautiful box containing the dress and shoes chosen by the sculptor. She stood behind a large black curtain to change while Mr. Dunbar readied his camera in front of a large open window overlooking the Savannah River. The dress was a vibrant peacock blue, not a color Virginia would have chosen. Outspoken and bold, the lovely costume was quite opposite the silent tans, blacks, and browns she usually wore. The satin shoes were dyed a perfect peacock blue to match.

Virginia removed her plain black blouse and white skirt, folded them neatly and placed them on the cane-back chair inside the curtain. She pulled the dress up over her waist and marveled at the material and fit. She turned like a ballerina, and the skirt ballooned to show off detailed embroidery at the hem. There was no mirror, so she ran her hand down the back of the dress making sure the zipper was straight before emerging from the black curtain.

Harlan's face brightened when he spotted her. The young photographer asked her to turn slowly, complimenting her as she exited the makeshift dressing room. He had arranged two cameras and a few lights on tripods. The photographer held her hand gently as she stepped up to pose on the low platform. "Look towards the river," he said. "Try to ignore the buildings. Envision that you're looking at a passing ship."

Virginia could not believe she was doing something so exciting. She had insisted on coming alone for fear she'd be too embarrassed with her mother watching. The photographer positioned her arms above her head and placed a red scarf in her hands. The slightly open window helped the scene, allowing a breeze to fill the scarf. Virginia thought of Florence Martus and smiled as if greeting a ship. She held still, watching her shadow against the window, amazed at how much the outline matched the artist's original sketch of their Waving Girl.

Mr. Dunbar clicked on and on, taking what sounded to Virginia like hundreds of photos. She was a movie star, a woman in love, looking for her lover on passing ships. Harlan moved her hips square with the camera, lifted her chin, and re-adjusted her pose several times.

She was sad to stop posing and pretending when he said, "Thank you. That was lovely. I think I have what I need." Virginia lowered her arms, rubbing away the ache of holding them over her head for so long. Mr. Dunbar invited her to sit. "You must be thirsty. Have some sweet tea."

Virginia brushed off the chair before sitting down, not wanting to stain the dress, which she was sure would be shipped back to Mr. de Weldon. They sat together on a tattered gold chaise that seemed to be the only chair in the room. Mr. Dunbar poured the tea from a thermos and sat so close that she smelled his aftershave. She scooted as far to the edge of the chaise as possible.

Virginia sipped her tea, deciding what to say to this professional man. She had only experienced one date and that was with Tom Merritt, a pimply faced real estate agent's son from Tybee. This man had traveled much more than Tom who, she doubted, had ever left Savannah. She was clueless as to what type of conversation was suitable.

Virginia kept her comments simple. "Thank you for asking me to pose." She looked at Mr. Dunbar when she said it, hoping he would share a story of his famous employer. The man before her wore a mask of evil. Taken aback by his wicked appearance, Virginia looked around the darkened space for the composed professional who had photographed her. Dunbar's eyes and lips curled in a sinister expression of want.

"You're quite a beautiful young lady," he said. The hairs on the back of her neck lifted in warning, and she attempted to stand. He grabbed her arm and the tea spilled across the lovely dress. She pulled away, "Please. No, Mr. Dunbar." His hands were everywhere at once. He leaned his weight against her arms and torso and the sound of tearing fabric exploded as cold air reached her chest. She pulled one hand free, clutching desperately at the bodice to keep the dress together. His hand found her neck and pushed her down as he hissed, "You're going to love this."

She had not noticed the dirtiness of his hands before. She counted the fissures in the gray nails that groped her as he slammed her against the wood platform. He raped her until the only light in the room was a single, crooked spotlight projecting a moonlike beam on the ceiling.

She lay motionless even after he stopped, afraid he would kill her if she moved. He did not look at her when he growled, "Get dressed and get out, whore."

Virginia limped to pull her clothing from the chair in the dressing area. She pulled the garments on, moving towards the massive sliding door. Her legs felt bloated and leaden. Her head pulsated and lolled from side to side as she left. Outside in the darkness, the gravel path that had welcomed her cut her bare feet. Moving away from the deserted row of warehouses, she fell and the pain disappeared.

Virginia woke with a gurgled choke, the first sound she'd made since Marianne found her sprawled out in a patch of weeds beside the low stone wall leading to the warehouse. Virginia had only made it fifteen feet from the makeshift studio before she collapsed into unconsciousness.

163

At home in her bed, her mother stared at her with devastated eyes. "Virginia. Oh, my God. I'm so sorry."

At first, Virginia was unsure why her mother was apologizing. Then it hit her, and she pulled her legs against her chest, embarrassed, nauseated, and writhing in a state of eternal filth.

"We will not speak a word of this. I love you. We'll just try to forget. I'm sorry...I didn't know, Virginia, how could I? I'm so sorry, my love."

Virginia touched her burning throat, realizing that she could not speak. It did not matter though, because she did not want to. In fact, she thought she might never speak again.

Chapter 36

March 6, 1970

Keeping the story out of the papers required two telephone calls. Marianne called the city editor at the newspaper, who hesitated but agreed not to report the story. "I don't want your club after me for ruining the whole project. They'd never let me be. Please give your daughter my best, Marianne. I'm sorry it had to be her." Marianne was curious who he thought it should have been. If only she'd refused the photographer's offer, none of this would have happened.

She also called the mayor, reminding him how important the Waving Girl statue would be for tourism. "If the story gets out, it will ruin my daughter, and I can assure you the statue will not be erected. Imagine how angry your constituents will be, especially the ones who donated. The money is spent, Mayor. There are no refunds. Therefore, I'm sure you will reiterate my wishes to the media and the police chief."

The police chief investigated the crime, handling the media like a circus parrot. "No comment. No comment. No comment."

The police discovered that the building Virginia went to with the supposed photographer was empty with no record of anyone renting the space for years. At the crime scene, they found a couple of film canisters, a cigarette butt, and the makeshift dressing room. They also discovered that someone had cut the deadbolt on the storage building.

Three months after the investigation, Marianne told only one Altrusa Club member the real reason for her hasty retirement. Candice Burgeon was not happy about stepping up to the presidency. Content to hold a well-respected, less time-consuming role in the club, she'd badgered Marianne to give her a reason. "What could possibly be so important that you and Virginia have to leave now? Can't you at least stay until the statue is done?"

Candice's outrage melted when Marianne explained that the photographer was a fraud, and not hired by the sculptor to photograph Virginia. "It was not a...professional experience."

Candice watched Marianne tear up and knew what had transpired.

"I think it best that Virginia get away for a while." Marianne could not look at Candice for the guilt she felt at not having thoroughly checked the photographer's background. "We are going to look at colleges in New York to get her mind off things."

A luncheon was planned to see them off, and Candice knew the moment she spotted Virginia, that the girl was pregnant. Candice hugged Virginia and Virginia shuddered.

"Good luck," Candice whispered, regretting the inadequacy of the sentiment.

Chapter 37

June 8, 1970

The phone rang several times before he picked up. "Hello, Mr. de Weldon, this is Chief Randolph from the Savannah Police Department. I'd like to talk to you about the crime related to the Altrusa Club contract."

Randolph stuttered slightly, uncomfortable speaking to the man responsible for the Iwo Jima statue. "I'm a great admirer of your work sir," the chief stalled, a little ashamed to be wasting the illustrious man's time with details of the rape.

"As you know, a young girl from the Altrusa Club was the victim of the crime in March. She was asked to pose for a photographer who claimed he was hired by you to photograph a model for the Waving Girl statue."

De Weldon stopped his work on the open mouth of Florence's collie to listen more intently. The Waving Girl sculpture was nearly complete and should be ready for plaster in just a week.

De Weldon was concerned by what the man from Savannah was insinuating. "Sir, I'm not sure I understand. I did not hire anyone to take photos of a model. The only photos from Savannah I have are the ones I took of the river bank myself in January."

"Yes, we spoke to your assistant in March, a Mr. Montao. You were in Malaysia, unreachable, he said. Told me you would be back this month. He assured me that you did not hire

Harlan Dunbar to photograph Virginia Senton. Just following up, I need your formal statement for the file."

"Yes, Montao...that baboon neglected to mention it." De Weldon was at once angry and concerned. "If a crime was committed, I will help in any way I can." De Weldon washed his hands, watching the gray swirl of the water circle down the studio drain.

"Marianne Senton, as you know, is the President of the Altrusa Club," the chief continued. "She asked that I keep things quiet to protect her daughter's reputation and the statue. So you don't have to trouble yourself about press coverage."

"Well that's...is she okay?" De Weldon sat as the gravity of the Chief's words settled in.

"No. I'm sorry your assistant did not tell you. There's no easy way to say this. A man calling himself Harlan Dunbar raped Virginia Senton. According to Marianne, he met with the Altrusa Club in March, claiming that he was hired by you to take pictures for the statue."

"Why didn't the club contact me to confirm the hire?" De Weldon's voice grew louder. "The young woman, will she be okay?"

"As well as can be expected, considering. It was pretty brutal. We figured he was a fraud, probably picked Virginia out of the newspaper. I just need your statement to complete the paperwork." Trying to lighten the tone, he threw in, "How's she looking, our Waving Girl?"

Absently, de Weldon replied, "Beautiful, almost ready for casting in Italy. Almost. Thank you for letting me know Chief, and please keep me informed of any progress in the investigation."

Felix looked at the woman he had been creating for so many months. From the initial modeling sculpture, to the one-and-a-half times life-size clay creation in front of him, she was a lovely representation of Savannah's Waving Girl and of the city's welcoming spirit.

Felix went back to work on the dog's face, the crime heavy in his imagination. Haunting images of a childhood among Austria's Gothic cathedrals, baroque palaces, and museums churned through his mind.

Forty years of North American success had not erased the pain of Felix's departure from his Austrian home in the volatile 1930s. As Nazi rule blossomed, Felix made his way around the world, opening his first studio in London, then moving to Canada before joining the U.S. Navy, and later, settling in Washington, D.C.

At sixty-three, Felix filtered the past with experienced eyes that raised guilty scars of Jewish survival. The news that Dunbar used his name for the diabolical crime gave his scars a fresh pulse. Even the usually soothing aroma of the earthen clay did not abate his growing anger. The deception was unthinkable.

Distracted, he set down the clay tool and looked for the newspaper announcement sent by Marianne Senton. He found it in the Waving Girl file and located Virginia in the photo. She was even younger than he'd expected, multiplying his outrage. He would write to her family.

Calling the club to obtain an address, de Weldon spoke to newly appointed President Candice Burgeon.

"It is tragic," she agreed with the artist, delighted to introduce herself to the celebrated sculptor and relieved that he already knew about the crime.

"Where might I send a note?" he asked.

Candice blurted out an answer to the simple question, "Marianne has gone to New York with Virginia, so she can have it there. So sad that the baby will have to be told this someday."

"Baby? You mean Virginia?" De Weldon was confused.

"Uh, no, I mean, they're having mail forwarded, so you can write them at West Perry Street, same postal code as the club. I'm glad to hear things are on schedule with the statue, good day, sir." She hung up, hoping de Weldon did not catch on, and if he did, that he would not expose her as the source of the information.

Felix realized that Virginia was not only raped but also pregnant. He looked at the address pondering what he would write to them. Looking at Florence's likeness, he decided to do something more significant.

Adding the forthcoming child to Florence's frame required only a little clay. Nestling the child among the folds of her skirt was effortless, and the result was subtle enough to remain invisible to anyone not looking for it.

As his hands worked the clay, de Weldon reflected on the baby's mother and stolen trust. The Senton girl thought she was modeling for him, and examining the slight protrusion he had created, he hoped it would help her to heal.

The note was not as easy as the artistic effort. No matter how many times he rewrote it, the words seemed meager in comparison with the gravity of the crime. The final version was short, and despite its inadequacy, he mailed it.

Chapter 38

June 16, 1991

L ara's hands fall to her lap. The silence is frigid and filled with a sadness deeper than the frantic cries of an abandoned baby, yearning for touch, care, and suckling.

Pearce watches as his niece absorbs the information in the letter, thinking of his sister's chronically worried state upon returning from New York. He had teased her for every cautious reprimand. "Mother, it seems we've got an old hen in the house. Virginia, why not let mother do the mothering?"

His sister was a mother after all. Thomas realizes that Virginia was a worried mother parenting him in place of the missing child she would never raise. It was this child, the one she gave away, who had caused his sister's perpetual worried looks, her constant wringing of hands, and her newly appeared, solemn maturity.

Virginia never left home after that trip. Thomas reflects on the hours she spent in the music room and how many times she must have reread the letters, agonizing about this girl. The music room was her refuge from the world that had let her down.

Virginia refused to participate in the community that set social standards that made it impossible for her to keep her child. Only now did Thomas understand why she'd ventured no farther than church, accepted no invitations regardless of how their mother peppered these with dating opportunities, fun, and freedom.

Recalling the look of immortal relief on Virginia's lifeless face at the funeral, it finally makes sense. All the days she lived after the relinquishment of her child had been torture. The severity of her admonishments, the hardness of her heart, the mean exterior she showed the world were all symptoms of having left Lara behind.

She must have found relief in death. Thomas believes she was finally free to watch over the baby who must have filled every waking thought.

"What is the Enchanted Violin?" Lara's whispered question brings him back to the child, the woman, his niece. The last line in Virginia's letter reads, "Justice will come from the Enchanted Violin."

"I'm not sure. I recall an antique shop named Violin something or other. I think it's on Bull Street."

The second letter is lighter in Pearce's hand. Lara is staring at it. She wants to read it, in hopes that it will erase what her birth mother wrote in the first. *Please God,* she prays silently, *no more pain. Please, Lord, let this letter bring something whole.*

She nods and Thomas hands her the second letter. This one is shorter and typed on thick, textured stationary. Looking at Pearce for a clue as to its content, she rubs the thatched crisscross of lines between thumb and pointer finger. There are no clues in her uncle's eyes.

There are heavy lines in the single typed page, as if the paper has been folded and unfolded hundreds of times.

Dearest Mrs. Senton,
It is with great sorrow that I pen this letter of condolence. I understand that a terrible crime was enacted on your

172

family and committed under the falsehood of employment by me.

I assure you the criminal was not in my employ and that I will do all I can to hasten his capture.

In reverence to your child and her treasure, I recalled them in my work. When you look to the statue, you will find the child sleeping in the bronze folds of your most gracious resident.

This small gesture is to be cast in the coming months, and I hope by that time, your family will find some manner of peace and healing.

Sincerely,
Felix de Weldon

The sculptor knew about her. He called her a treasure. Surely, her mother and grandmother did not see her as that. Her birth ruined Virginia's life. She was a curse to the Pearce family, and half of her lineage was more evil than anything she had imagined.

Lara runs to the bathroom and vomits. Thomas stands outside the bathroom, feeling ineffective and unsure as to what to do for her. When she finally emerges, red-faced and smacking her lips at the foul taste of all that has come up, he says, "You should rest, Lara. You must be in shock. I know I am."

Carefully considering which room to let her lie down in, Thomas chooses Virginia's. He has not slept at all after opening the ninth drawer. He shudders at the magnitude of her turmoil.

He hopes that Lara will find enough of his sister there to ease some of the loss and shock.

Lara's head spins on the pillow as the ceiling fan swooshes into action, stirring the white lace curtains of her birth mother's room. She tosses and turns exhausted, praying the room is a dream. The nauseating truth burns her eyes open and forces them closed again. Even sleep cannot extinguish the hard wall of knowing.

In her dreams, Virginia holds her like an infant, rocking her too-large self on her lap. They rock until the chair falls away and they are on a dusty, wooden platform. A bloodstained scarf floats around their necks, tangling and tightening. Her arms ache as she holds onto her birth mother, but the scarf tightens again, yanking her away. Virginia reaches, and their fingers touch momentarily, until Lara is tossed across the blackened room. When she looks back, Virginia is gone.

Chapter 39

June 17, 1991

A patch of sunlight illuminates the closet door, transposing the stems and leaves of the lace curtains. *Where am I?* It takes Lara a minute to recall where she is and for the angry burn of her violent beginning to return. A photo of her birth mother sits on the white dresser. It takes only a moment for her to realize that she is in her birth mother's room. Sitting up and taking a tissue from the nightstand to blow her nose, she is taken aback by her uncle's choice of accommodation.

The grief that shocked Lara into sleep's sweet escape was brought on by the description of her birth mother's rape and the painful tearing away of her newborn self. She was wanted, but they took her away. Lara digests the truth again, staring at another photo on the dresser. It is of her birth mother and grandmother. Marianne's betrayal was hateful. Despite their blood ties, Lara was a filthy creature who warranted abandonment. The father, the rapist, made her a dirty secret to hide.

Virginia wrote that she should not be angry with the family, that they were protecting her reputation. Lara imagines her grandmother's stern face instructing the nurses to take her from Virginia. Lara frowns deeply, picturing Virginia's weakened state after her birth. With the fight ripped from her by rape and fate, it is a miracle that that she had the strength to write the letter and hide it. When she had asked the hospital photographer for help, he must not have known the severing to come.

Virginia never married. The frivolity of living ended with the rape and the relinquishment of her child. She remained half-alive, the need to nurture the child gone from her reach forever haunting her. Instead of the intended social fortification, Marianne's decision to leave her granddaughter in a New York hospital froze Virginia's life in a purgatory of empty-armed torment.

Finally revealed, the pain her birth mother endured incubates easily in its living source. Lara is sitting in her birth mother's bed, enduring the evaporation of imagined endings. There will be no laughter, no lunches, and no common ground to explore.

As adoption labels fade, new places and faces reprint the fabric of her identity. These replacements baffle her core. Finding was supposed to define, not derange her sense of self. Familiar is no longer true. Her adoptive mother's face and the stack of photo albums in the hall closet of her New York home are memories cast in barbed metal. A new molten reality threatens to absorb them as they pass through her seared heart.

She had slept much of the day. Signs of her uncle's check-ins include a bowl of untouched soup and a glass of water on the bedside table. The bedcovers appear tangled and tossed from her fitful sleep. She is thirsty and needs a shower.

Her birth mother's room still holds many of Virginia's things. A silver brush and mirror, and an unopened oriental fan rest on a mirrored tray next to a framed photo. Lara looks for evidence of Virginia, touching each item, trying to feel a connection in them, but there are no strands of hair in the bristles of the brush and the mirror, polished to perfection. The birth and death registers she'd searched in the library proved that every life leaves behind a tuggable thread. Lara heads to the closet to find hers.

A surprising number of wardrobe items hang there, most covered in garment bags. They look like a mix of clothing from her grandmother and mother. Stylish suits and floral dresses intermingle with plain sheaths and linen slacks. Opening each bag and pulling garments from useless storage, Lara puts her nose to one after the other, seeking a hint of her mother's scent. If only she can smell Virginia, maybe she will feel her too, but mothballs and plastic are all she inhales as she hugs the clothes, crying again for all that is lost.

Thomas's light knock hastens her re-zipping of the garment bags. Lara washes her face in the tiny washroom and brushes her hair back from her face. "Come in."

Thomas carries a prepared tray of fruit, juice, coffee and buttered toast into Virginia's room. Despite hours of rest, Lara can tell by her uncle's sympathetic expression that she looks as haggard and as spent as she feels. She attempts a half-grin hoping to relieve her uncle's concern. Lara looks at her uncle and finds that her nose is quite like his. He smiles too, yet neither can find the right words. Thomas puts the tray down on the bed. "Lara, I'm glad you found me. I know you're heartbroken, but I'm glad you're here. I only wish…"

"Mr. Pearce, I'm glad to know," she hesitates, "all of it. It's just gonna take some time to digest."

"You may call me Uncle if you wish." Smoothing the covers, he sits at the edge of the bed and extends his hand to her.

A half smile emerges from the strained muscles of her face. "I'd like that."

After another awkward silence, lacking a single suitable syllable, Lara finds her voice. "I'm a mess. I'd better get back to the hotel."

"About that," he interrupts. "I think you should check out today. I'll have a car pick up your things if you like. I think it's appropriate, considering all of this." Thomas indicates the room, the house, and newly exposed truth as his reasoning. "I don't think it's proper for you to be staying at a hotel when… Well, I hope you'll stay here."

Lara looks around the room where Virginia suffered after the loss of her baby. Pearce assumes her silence is trepidation. "Lara, if you're uncomfortable in her room, we can choose another. I just thought you might want to—"

"No. I'd like to stay in her room, if you're sure," Lara answers, content to have a place where she belongs.

With welcome extended and a move decided upon, Lara insists on going back to the hotel herself. It is where her journey started, and she feels the urge to say a proper farewell. Besides, she has two important stops to make today, and she wants to make them alone.

Chapter 40

June 16, 1991

The light on her phone flashes and there are three messages asking her to call the front desk. Rather than waste the call, she will handle the issue on the way out. Hoping she doesn't owe anything, she counts the bills in her wallet. There's only three hundred and twenty-five dollars left of the loan money, enough to get home.

The glass ceiling of the hotel gleams under a fierce sun. Lara's suitcase is heavier than she remembers. She lugs it, along with her backpack, to the front desk. A woman with the lovely British lilt asks her to wait. From an alcove behind the reception desk, the clerk brings a basket of wildflowers. Another hotel employee follows with a dozen perfect white roses arranged in an amber vase.

"Can we bring these to your car, ma'am?" the petite Brit asks.

"No, thank you." She knows they are from Robert. Curious, she opens the enclosure cards attached to each arrangement. The first reads, "Where have you been? I miss you. Love, Robert." The second, "Please call me."

She lifts the heavy vase of roses and places it on the tourist information table to her left. They complement the dark wood beautifully. Lara hands the second arrangement back to the woman behind the desk. "Enjoy." The little lady is surprised and thanks Lara for the impromptu gift.

Lara signs the checkout form, relieved to see that her early departure will result in a refund. Lara shoves the forms into the front of her pack, resuming the back-aching process of getting her cases to the car. She is almost at the parking elevator when she hears her name. "Miss Lara, ya sure got me earning my keep this week."

Abel is leaning against the wall near the elevator, winded and dwarfed by an immense arrangement of red roses and lavender. A young couple waits near him, wearing white baseball caps with the words "bride" and "groom" embroidered on them. Abel holds the arrangement out to Lara. She takes it, plucks the card from the plastic stick, and hands the flowers to the bride saying, "Congratulations."

Lara reads the card. "We need to talk. Please call me."

Abel flashes a golden smile, exaggerating a sigh. "That Robert's not going to give up easy. He has been calling every day. You done with him then?" Abel asks, pointing at the flowers now heading down the elevator with the bride.

"Yes, Abel," Lara hugs him. "Thank you for bringing them. If you get any more, would you send them to someone who needs cheering up? Don't tell who they're from though, okay?"

"Sure enough. I have a few elderly friends who'd be thrilled to get them. Plus, I might get a couple of home-cooked meals out of it."

"You were right, Abel. I never really said thank you, but you were right all along. I saw him with another tourist, you know, switching things up."

"Figured as much. I'm sorry."

"Don't be. I understand why he does it. He's a hurt little boy. Anyway, I have had some sort of good news. I found my Savannah connection."

"You found your family then?" Abel touches his hand to his heart, pinky extended and lets out a whopping, "Hallelujah."

180

Lara feels safe sharing with Abel. He is eccentric and good. His warnings about Robert taught a crucial life lesson. Goodness lives in unexpected places. Lara recalls how she feared Abel at first because of his appearance. Yet, like Miss Susan, Abel is so much more. Now she knows that it was not their appearances that made her want to shrink away. It was her insecurity. Lara decides that there is goodness in the world and that rape, abuse, or death does not define her. There is good.

"I found my mother's brother. I'll be staying with him for a while." Lara tells Abel all that has happened since they last met. She recalls the highs and lows in muted tones, still unsure how to feel about all of it.

"Guess I better say goodbye now." As she says it, Lara realizes the dread is gone. The prospect of leaving Savannah is easier to contemplate. "Not sure how long before I head back to New York."

"You'll be back, ya know." Abel sounds confident. "Pleasssssse call me when you come back, Miss Lara. This old heart will stop if you don't." Abel mimes the beating of a heart on his thin chest. Lara laughs. "Better make it fast too, 'cause business has never been better." They part with a smile.

Lara heaves the bags into the trunk of her car. With just her shoulder bag in tow, she walks from the garage toward the river. Her pace increases to a trot when she spots the green of Florence's skirt peeking through the trees.

Blessedly alone, she stands in front of the Waving Girl again, studying her wavy hair and ample bosom. Almost afraid to find it missing, she looks to the folds of fabric depicted at the waist. Down a bit further is the treasure. Easily missed, but blessedly there, it is as plain to see as the sweat dripping from her forehead. She is there below the folds of metal, a violent pregnancy cast with dignity. Her birth has been marked and hidden for eternity.

A few long strides and a bit of maneuvering and she is standing on the base of the statue. On tippy toes, Lara touches the swell of metal. The pregnancy is unmistakable among the breezy folds of the bronze skirt. The warmth of the metal under her fingers is nearly unbearable as she rubs the belly repeatedly.

Lara wants to lay her head against the stomach wrought in her honor, but the statue is too tall. Turning to get down, she finds a couple watching her. They are waiting to take a picture of the statue. She hops down, slightly embarrassed, yet elated to be privy to the secret. Like so many before them, the couple will never know what is right before their eyes.

"They rub Buddha's belly for good luck," she says, excusing herself and backing up to let the tourists take a picture. The intoxicating aroma of gardenia wafts over her, the river swells in the wake of a passing yacht, and a forever memory is made.

Chapter 41

June 17, 1991

"How many one-way streets are there in this city?" Lara is driving past the chocolatier for the seventh time. The confection-laden window becomes more intriguing with each pass. The map says she is on Monterey Square and that the shop is definitely on Bull Street, but she has yet to see it.

On this approach, she slows to a crawl and merges to the right, allowing anxious drivers enough room to pass. Finally, she spots it, partially hidden by a long construction scaffold. Passing the Pulaski monument and luxuriant greenery of the picturesque square three more times, she finally lands a parking spot.

To the left of the door is an exquisite garden angel. Her white wings billow downward, her tranquil expression ruined only by the considerable price tag resting in her arms. Lara enters the Enchanted Violin, the same shop named in her birth mother's letter, without an inkling as to what she's looking for.

All of the clues in the Bible letter are unraveled. The Enchanted Violin was important to Virginia though and so, in her honor, Lara is here. Pushing past an old spinning wheel, she spots what appears to be a service desk backed into a pantry whose once neat shelves have given way to a mass of unusual, dust-covered relics.

The keys of the faded brass cash register reach out like over-extended skeleton digits, waiting for someone to tuck them back into the casing. Four drawers hold whatever monetary gains the tiny place might earn. Lara eyes with some amusement an emerald brooch pinned to a beret someone tossed on the point of a glass-eyed, mounted deer head.

Lara's pant cuff rubs against something scratchy as she squeezes closer to the counter, and whatever she unhinged clatters to the uneven floorboards. Bending to retrieve the item, she hopes it's not broken. "Clumsy oaf," she scolds herself.

"Hello," a husky voice calls from the back corner of the shop. As he moves towards her, Lara picks up the cane she spilled from its resting place against the counter. She recognizes the ivory inlay of chrysanthemums and the voice. It is Artimar Pace, the man from Laurel Grove cemetery.

She holds the cane for a bit too long and he asks, "My dear, will you watch me limp all day?"

Lara hands the cane over, and he instantly leans on it for support. "I'm sorry, sir. I hope it's not damaged."

"No, little lady, looks fine to me. Something I can help ya find?"

Artimar doesn't recognize her. She must look different, devoid of the outrage and grave dust. At least she hopes so.

"Just browsing." She does not remind him of their last meeting. *He might be senile or something.*

"Help yourself. I'll be just over there sorting out them books. Someone left them at the back door last night. Darned lucky it didn't rain; some nice leather there. We get all kinds of donated items. Some of it's junk, but now and again, I luck out. One man's trash, ya know."

"Yes, sir." Lara heads in the opposite direction, poking around a china cabinet stuffed with sugar bowls and a mishmash of china plates. A collection of vintage dresses catches her eye, and Lara lifts the frayed remnants of a beaded flapper dress, imagining a gloved, smoking lady in it. At the opposite end of the shop, she spies a zebra-patterned ottoman and recalls the Mercury club. This one looks real. She is disgusted to know that some savage killed a zebra, just for a place to put their feet.

After perusing a box of World War II photographs, a box of thick 78-speed records, and some beaded purses, Lara goes back to the register to look at the brooch she was reaching for when she toppled Artimar's cane.

Artimar is behind the counter now, pricing the books donated from parts unknown.

"Find any treasure?" he asks without looking up.

"How much is the brooch?" she asks, indicating the beret.

"Costume you know," Artimar answers, "How about ten dollars?"

"Perfect." Lara puts her backpack on the counter and searches for her wallet among her unruly collection of maps and brochures.

Artimar uses his cane to retrieve the beret and he frees the pin. "You from out of town?"

She is about to answer when he recognizes her. "Why, you're the girl from the cemetery? Pearce, right?

"Guilty." Artimar's memory is pretty decent after all. Lara hopes he will remember why Virginia mentioned his shop.

"Well, it's nice to see you, young lady. How's the search progressing? Need any help from a rare antique?" Artimar smiles. Lara imagines he is happy at the prospect of conversation and company. How long can a man stand being alone amidst a growing stockpile of old things?

"I wasn't sure you'd remember. I might need your help after all. I found my family. My birth mother was Virginia Senton. Have you heard of her?"

"No, can't say I have. Did you say 'was'? Passed on?" Artimar frowns sympathetically.

"Yes, sir. Do you happen to have anything here related to the Waving Girl statue?"

"Hmm, don't think so. I usually keep anything like that up here to catch a few tourist sales."

Lara looks at the ice skates, hatboxes, and boxes of postcards stacked on the counter and wonders where such a tourist display might fit. "Thanks anyway." Lara finds her wallet and before paying, she notices a camera. Hoofing through Savannah has offered hundreds of photo opportunities and yet she has not taken even one.

"It'd be a sin to leave Savannah without some photos for my mom's scrapbook. May I see that?" Lara asks, pointing to the camera.

Artimar hands it over. The lens cap has a deep scratch, but the lens appears to be intact. The black housing has a gouge, as well, as if keyed or pulled along something sharp.

"Looks abused," Lara says.

Artimar agrees. "It's pretty old, my stepson left it when he moved, probably twenty years ago. Not even sure it works. Take it if you want it. Consider it a going-away present."

"Let me pay you something."

"I insist, take it," Artimar says.

Lara pays for the brooch and thanks him.

"Still have my card?" he asks.

"Sure do," she replies, hoping he does not ask for it back since she has no idea where it is.

"Good, if you get that old camera working, send me a photo of the Statue of Liberty. Been meaning to get up your way to see that old gal."

"I will." She shakes Artimar's hand, and he lifts it to his lips to kiss it.

"Have a safe trip."

Toting the war-worn camera under her arm and wearing her new brooch, Lara heads back to the car.

Chapter 42

June 17, 1991

Miss Susan scolds her like a schoolgirl, "Young lady, when I called the hotel and they said you checked out, I was sick. After the rat dance you had with Robert, I was sure you'd packed up and gone home."

Susan is uncharacteristically silent as Lara fills her in on her family. Three times, she has to ask her if she's on the line.

"Uh huh," is her reply.

When Lara finishes Susan finally speaks, "So is your uncle available?"

Lara laughs, and then spots a woman in a uniform, heading towards her car. "Uh oh, meter maid. I'm in for it. Gotta run. Plus, I'm out of change for the phone. I promise not to wait so long before calling again. I'm staying at the Pearce's, in Virginia's old room."

"Seen her yet?"

"What?"

"Well, if what they say about tormented souls becoming ghosts, that mother of yours is Casper's queen."

"Thanks a lot. I'll be up all night."

"Okay, girl. Keep in touch."

Lara runs, arriving just in time to avoid a ticket.

Back at her uncle's, Lara finds a note taped to the door. "Sorry, meeting. Key is under the bluest flower."

She chuckles at the idea of another family riddle, looking at each flower in the front bed and wondering which might be deemed "bluest." There are a few African blue irises, but the clear winner is the powder blue hydrangea growing in the shade of the magnolia. Under the bush, she finds a key box buried in the mulch. Lara smiles at how simply she found the key, deciding her mother was a far better riddler than her uncle is.

With a new sense of kinship and confidence, Lara enters her first family's home, the place her birth mother was so keen on having her find. While the circumstances of her birth were tragic, Virginia looked past it to give her the selfless gift of a heritage.

Lara has never hidden her adopted status.

"Be glad you lost the bitch," one friend suggested at the mention of a possible search. Her abandonment made people angry with the woman who ditched her. "She didn't want you. Why do you want to know her?" they would ask.

Despite these comments, Lara never cast the unknown mother as detestable. Realistic about the possibility of a negative outcome, Lara never hated the woman who gave her away. Instinct told her that she was wanted.

Now Lara has found her truth, and it drips with unexpected malevolence. Not Virginia, but her birth father is a villain. A hateful creation, she is a part of a monster but feels a union with her birth mother's side. Survival is all about aligning yourself with the lesser evil.

Setting her bags on the neatly made bed, Lara looks at the room with more clarity than the first time she saw it. The previous owner has settled into her heart, a new sliver of identity. She is not discoverable by touch; Lara must find her in memories and place.

Looking for hints of Virginia in the wall decor, curtains, and lace-edged bed skirt, Lara decides her birth mother was a romantic. There are no photos other than Virginia's portrait. There are no postcards to tell of travels, no books to tell of preferences or stories known. Other than the décor, the room is lifeless.

Lara wants to peek into the drawers of the dresser for more clues, yet wonders at the correctness of the invasion. Guessing that her uncle had it cleaned out years ago, she touches the brass hardware of the white bedside stand.

Deciding that her birth mother would not mind a sliver of intrusion, she slides the drawer forward just far enough to see that it is empty except for a white bobby pin, decorated with three tiny rhinestones. She takes the barrette and pins it in her hair, hoping it belonged to her mother. Turning to the long dresser, she bargains again for just an inch. The drawers are empty. There is nothing more to find here.

Roaming the large house, Lara views photos of Virginia at different ages. Each room is elaborately decorated, from the sculpted ceilings to the large Asian rugs and oil paintings. The opulent staircase is worthy of a princess, leading to all three levels of the home.

Lara is sitting in a gold-tufted bedroom chair on the third floor when Thomas comes home. Setting his keys on the table near the door, he calls her, "Lara, are you here?"

She leaves the cushy contemplation of the room to lean over the thick iron rail and yell, "Yes, up here."

Thomas greets her cordially but his presence makes Lara's insecure. She pictures how she must have looked to him, while throwing up in his gold-plated sink and wonders if she should apologize for the drama.

"Did you get checked out of the hotel?" Thomas asks.

"Yes, and I visited the Enchanted Violin."

"So soon? Anything of interest?"

"Not really, just this old camera." Lara points to the camera on the hall table. "I haven't taken any photos of Savannah."

"Well, then, a smart buy. Does it work? Mind if I have a look?"

"Of course not." Lara hands Thomas the camera. He examines the dents and scratches on the camera's housing. "I may have an extra camera lying around if this one turns out to be a dud."

"Thanks, I'll get some film tonight."

"One sec, I might have a roll of thirty-five millimeter in my camera bag."

"Perfect. I'll try it out first thing tomorrow."

Thomas examines the camera further, turning the winding mechanism and pulling forward the tiny lever to open the back. At first, the film door sticks, but a quick shake loosens it, and it opens to reveal a roll of film still in its chamber.

"Look here, comes with film. Too bad it's used."

Lara laughs. "Maybe a tourist took photos of Savannah for me. It'll be fun to get developed." Lara pops the roll into her pocket. A shared endeavor, examination of the camera, eases the awkward newness of the relationship.

Thomas is relieved that his hand does not shake as he fiddles with the camera. Still off balance from the idea of his sister's pregnancy, he wishes there was a woman to help him say the right things in this highly unusual circumstance. Nothing in his life has prepared him for the proper handling of this situation.

His mother had insight into his sex's inability to handle the emotions surrounding an unwanted pregnancy. Thomas believes she was protecting him when she failed to tell him what happened to Virginia. When Virginia died, Thomas regretted the things she missed. He thought her life to be secluded and dull. To die young without a husband or children to carry the light forward made her death more tragic.

If only his mother had shared the child's existence. He would have spared no expense in trying to locate her. Thomas's mother died only four years after Virginia, leaving him quite alone. Social engagements and friends filled the time, but he sorely missed his family. Marrying for companionship became an option twice in his early thirties, and he'd opted out, claiming the burden of business responsibilities to be wife enough.

Now facing the girl who looks so like Virginia, he wonders how to embrace her without scaring her off. Wanting to welcome but not overwhelm her, he flounders in silence, trying to find a proper word to utter.

Lara is also at a loss for words as the camera conversation ends. She stands there shuffling one foot across the oriental runner and watches the pile of the carpet transform from dark to light.

"Are you hungry?" Thomas asks.

"Always," Lara answers.

"Would you like to get something at the Pink House?"

"Uh, would you mind if we went somewhere else?" She does not want the memory of the dinner with Robert to ruin her first night out with her uncle.

"Sure. There's a new place over at the Best Western I've been meaning to try. I heard the lady makes killer fried chicken."

"Great," Lara agrees.

"We'll drop off your film on the way," Thomas says.

"Oops, sorry." Lara drops the film canister as she escapes the overwhelming waft of processed leather in his meticulous car. The canister rolls under the car, and Thomas gallantly retrieves it, staining the knee of his pants in the process.

"Sorry." She says it four more times before they reach the photo shop near the hotel restaurant. Lara is nervous about what she will discuss with her new uncle. Dinner will be torture if they run out of things to say.

Thomas waits while Lara runs into the store to drop off the now grimy film canister. Pickup is any time after noon the next day.

The fried chicken is golden and looks almost good enough for a taste. Lara has loaded her plate with mashed potatoes, greens, and salad. She watches Thomas inhale mac and cheese and regrets not getting some from the ample buffet.

Thomas goes up three times and Lara wonders if appetite is an inherited trait. She joins him for two helpings of the richest, cheesiest, most butterlicious macaroni and cheese ever and considers unbuttoning her jeans. Her Italian grandfather did it after every meal. However, this is not New York, and Thomas would probably pass out.

Chapter 43

June 17, 1991

"Drink, Lara?" Her uncle pours scotch from a crystal decanter.

Not sure if she can stomach the stuff, Lara declines. Food filled the nooks and crannies of missing conversation at dinner. They discussed Virginia's doll collection and how she forced Thomas to join her teatime fun. Thomas explained, "She thought each doll was a member of the royal family and I was court jester."

The fact that she'll never know Virginia is like lead in Lara's heart. She will never hear the sound of her voice. *Was it raspy, soft, or southern?* Maureen's heavy New York accent is commonplace. Lara has heard it cry, scream, soothe, and whisper of dreams, worries, and hopes. Virginia's voice is second-hand silence. Only through Thomas will she come to imagine it.

Home and her mother's possible reactions are on her mind. The uncovering of secrets has worried Maureen from the moment she found the cryptic note with Lara's baby photo. "Some things are better left alone," Maureen's protective mantra, plays in Lara's head. There is no cushion thick enough to brace her mother for the impact.

A rapist father and a family with financial means, Lara's heritage plays like a roll call of Maureen's worst imaginings. Only the fact that her birth mother is dead will soften the blow. There will be no sharing of the mother role.

Lara considers heading home wrapped in a made-up tale of failure. Her extended family would rally at such news, delivering a well-intended "told you so," and easing Lara back into a rhythm of normalcy.

Denial is not a real option though. Savannah and Thomas are a part of her now. Virginia and the horrible man who raped her are a significant part of the new reality. Watching her uncle sip the bronze liquid as he reads the newspaper, Lara questions if she will ever find a balance between before and after. Her great-great-grandfather's morality is a part of her. Her grandmother's historical fortitude is there as well. The mapping of each inherited trait will take years.

Thomas interrupts her thoughts. "It may not be my place, but have you told your adoptive family about…this?"

"I will," Lara says, "I'm not sure what to say though. My mother, the other one, I mean Mom, she'll be upset. I might wait 'til I get home."

"You're welcome to stay here as long as you want. I'd enjoy showing you some of the family places in Savannah."

"I'd like that. I think I'll stay a couple more days. I'd like to see Savannah without looking for a needle in every haystack. You know, just enjoy the scenery."

"Wonderful. We'll start tomorrow."

The questions Lara asked him at dinner would fill a thousand White House press conferences. Thomas wants to answer as many of them as possible before she leaves. He wants her to know about his sister's childhood, her grandparents' achievements, and more about the family business, which barring his having children, will be hers.

The house feels happier with the re-introduction of conversation, and Thomas dreads its return to stillness. Discussion mingles with memories well past midnight, and each learns the lessons from a different world. By the time they head to their rooms, each sees with new eyes. They hug goodnight as blood begins to bond.

Lying once again in Virginia's room, Lara reflects on what is lost and found. *Blood connects us, but that alone does not make us family.* It's knowing that her uncle scratches his left eyebrow when he recalls something important, and how his eyes brighten from gray to green when he talks about kicking Virginia out of his childhood room and booby-trapping the door. Sharing will make them family.

Chapter 44

June 18, 1991

On a second sunny morning, Lara wakes in her biological mother's room. This day she feels like she could sleep forever. The digital clock reads 10:38. In the real world, it is late. She rises to push away the covers and then falls back on the down pillow, realizing she does not having a blessed thing to do. There are no more clues to follow. She is done. Hugging the pillow hard to muffle a squeal of delight, Lara revels in the lightness of a jigsaw piece, once lost, then found and put in its proper place.

Still, she does not want her uncle to consider her lazy, so she manages a shower. Sniffing at the vanilla soap, she speculates if her birth mother used the brand. Drying her hair at the vanity, Lara imagines how many times Virginia sat in this exact spot doing the same.

With her uncle at a "must-attend" morning meeting, Lara attempts a slide down the banister only to find that iron rails have painful ridges. "Ow." She rubs her bottom on the way to the kitchen where a covered tray on the stove reveals cinnamon French toast. "Yum." Pouring generic brand bran flakes into a red plastic bowl at home is going to be tough after this gourmet treatment.

Covering the toast in syrup, Lara decides to spend the day taking photos of all the places she will tell her mother about. After calling Susan to invite her along, Lara uses a sponge to blot at the syrup she's dripped on her only clean shirt. She wore the same shirt when she met Robert. "Perhaps a ritual burning is in order," she announces unenthusiastically.

Removing a ticket from her dirty windshield and tossing it in the backseat, Lara remembers that she needs film. Heading to the shop where she left the mystery roll for developing, she finds a spot two cars from the door. "Sweet," she says.

Ringing her up for film and processing, the pony-tailed photo clerk says, "You have some pretty cool photos there. You an art student?"

"Nope," Lara is intrigued. "Mind if I open them here?" she asks.

"No problemo."

She tears open the envelope, revealing about twenty sepia-toned photos. Most are blurred, thumb-over-the-lens beauties. One grainy picture is of the ocean through a window. The next is a woman's shapely legs. "Artsy all right," she reviews sarcastically. The next photo is the back of a woman: same legs, big skirt, and her hands over her head and holding something outside the range of the photo.

Flipping quickly through the rest, Lara finds nothing of interest. The last three pictures in the pile are gray and black nothingness.

"Interesting. Thanks again." Lara sticks the photos back in the envelope and into her purse, hoping that today's shots turn out better.

Susan is waiting on the sidewalk in front of a mansion.

"Finally. Thought you'd never get here. This woman is giving me the heebie-jeebies. See her up there? She's in one of her fourteen bedrooms, spying like I'm 'bout to steal the geraniums out of the window boxes."

"Fourteen bedrooms?" Lara jokes. "Poor thing, how does she decide where to sleep?"

"Heck with her," Susan replies. "Poor housekeeper, 'magine washing sheets for fourteen beds."

"So, want to see my pre-natal likeness first?" Lara asks.

"Sure, I'll look at pregnant metal bellies all day, so long as you feed me."

"Didn't think I'd be parking in here again," Lara says as they drive into the Marque garage. Bypassing the lobby, they walk the steep sidewalk to the riverfront. Susan trips over a shift in the cement.

"Drink much?" Lara teases.

The Waving Girl is her usual shiny self when Susan climbs up to rub her belly in tribute. Lara takes her first Savannah photos. Each is perfectly posed and gorgeous: Susan rubbing the Waving Girl's belly, Susan panting next to the collie, a few of the statue alone. Lara frames the handkerchief in her viewfinder, capturing Florence from every angle.

"Oh, my God!" Lara shrieks, catching the attention of a group of tourists who turn away from the river to locate the source of the tumult.

Susan jokes, "Getting some good baby portraits? Ya look a little green round the gills."

Lara, frozen, is staring.

"What's up, girl? Bee bit ya tongue?"

Lara turns, grabs Susan's hand, and hurries her down the steps. Susan fumbles again on the uneven pavement as Lara charges forward, pulling Susan for a while, and then releases her hand to move faster. The camera sways and bobs on her neck.

What in the world? Susan grumbles, "I'm starved. It is ninety-five degrees out here, and I'm running. What is this, the Army?" Susan attempts to move elegantly as she hurries after Lara, waving at the wide-eyed tourists. Lara is a good fifteen feet ahead when she turns into the garage and disappears. "Dang, that girl ought to run a marathon," Susan murmurs at passing pedestrians.

When Susan finally reaches the parking garage, she spots the interior light of Lara's car. The driver side door is open. Lara's legs are outside the car, her body stretched toward the back seat. From the passenger side, Susan sees Lara's horrified face. She is holding a stack of black and white photos, some strewn across the back seat and a few are on the floor next to her purse.

Susan opens the passenger door and what she sees in Lara's eyes is horror. "Lara, you look like you seen the devil himself."

Lara stares at the photo in her hand. Susan can barely make out the details but it looks like a girl being held up. Her face is blurry. Her arms up. Lara looks at Susan, and whispers two words, "My mother."

The realization continues to erupt, disjointed, impossible. *Maybe this is one of my nightmares,* Lara hopes, dismissing the thought when she feels Susan's hand rubbing her back. "It's okay. Whatever it is, you'll be okay, Lara."

"No. It's her. This is when I, when he. How can I be holding this?" Staggered gasps of panic explode from her lungs.

"Where on earth did you get photos of your mama?" Susan is sweaty and confused, but focuses on mollifying Lara. "Girl, you gotta calm down 'fore you give ya'self a dang stroke."

Lara lies motionless, legs out of the car, belly against the seat, her hand clamped on a photo. For Lara, the world has fallen from its axis. Unable to assimilate what she is seeing as real, her mind repeats a dull mantra of disbelief. *This is not happening. This cannot be happening.* Flipping through the stack again, Lara winces at each dark image. The legs, no longer anonymous, appear below what looks like a dressing room curtain. Odd angles expose furniture, a wood platform, an innocent, posing amid promises of honor that will ruin her.

Suddenly repulsed by the shiny papers, she drops the photos to join the others on the car floor. "How?" Lara asks the question aloud as if the photographs will answer. "The camera."

Examining the deep marks on its surface, she realizes that each scar is evidence of the life-giving crime. The camera was his. Sitting up and closing the car door, she looks at Susan who is closing her door.

199

"This was my father's camera." Shaking her head, desperate to wake from what has to be a nightmare, Lara watches Susan collect the photos from the floor.

Lara tries to remember what Artimar said, penetrating the mental vortex of images. "He said something about it belonging to a son? A stepson? I have to talk to him...now."

Racing past the Cotton Exchange, she nearly turns up a one-way street in an effort to get to the shop. Susan is shouting directions and holding onto the handle above her door. Lara takes the next turn, circles past the chocolatier, and speeds around the square. "No parking spots, of course."

Lara pulls close to a car parked in front of the Enchanted Violin and, leaving the car running, rushes towards the shop. Susan hurries to the driver's side, watching to see where Lara headed. Once Lara enters the shop, Susan takes off to find a parking place.

Jostled by her entrance, a tiny bell announces Lara's arrival. She stands just inside, catching her breath, while her eyes adjust to the dim interior. Rushing past the clutter of once treasured items to the alcove where the old register resides, she spots Artimar on his knees, holding a dustpan filled with the broken glass of what used to be a lavender platter.

"Well, hello again. Back with my Liberty photos so soon?" Artimar winks at her, grabbing his cane to stand.

"No. The camera. Where did you get it?" The words come out as an accusation. The volume of her inquisition halts Artimar's ascent.

"Doesn't work? It figures. My stepson was never good at taking care of things. I might have another you can have."

"No. The camera had film in it." Lara rushes at Artimar, grabbing his shoulders and pushing her face close to his. "Who is your stepson?"

"My, my, are you okay? You look a fright. Would you like to sit down, dear?" Artimar gestures to the stool beside him.

Realizing that she is frightening him, Lara sits and waits for an answer.

"My stepson is Harlan Dunbar. Likes to be called Kirk. That kid was a mess. Got his nickname in jail. He did three months in South Carolina for bad checks. Least that's what he said. One of the other inmates thought he looked like Captain Kirk. You know, *Star Trek*. Well, it stuck."

"It's him," Lara screeches, recalling that Dunbar was the name the photographer used. "Where is he now?" Lara snarls.

"Really, miss, would you like water or anything? You seem mighty upset." Susan arrives, heels in hand, just in time to hear the rest. "That roustabout left back in the seventies. I was only married to his mother one year before she passed. Harlan stayed with me for about six months after that. Never cared for him really. His mother loved him though, and I was pretty devastated after losing her. Never thought I'd get another chance at marriage. Guess I was right.

"After she died, I told him he could stay as long as he liked. He barely spoke to me the whole time he was living upstairs. He had the top floor. Three bedrooms up there. Plenty of room for us to avoid each other."

"Why'd he leave?" Lara knows the answer but wants to hear what Artimar believes was the reason. *What excuse did his sorry ass use to get away?*

"Never knew. Just noticed the groceries not getting eaten. He was a milk lover for sure, so when the gallon stayed full for a few days, I went up to check on him. He was gone. Nothing left but a couple of cameras, some books, and newspapers. One of the cameras was smashed to bits, I threw that one away. That one I gave you looked salvageable, so I added it to the mess down here.

"Why do you want to know about Harlan? Truth is, I was happy to find him gone. That kid had the kind of eyes that make my stomach churn. Nothing genuine behind them."

"There was film in his camera. Bad photos. I believe your stepson raped my mother." Hate swells in her stomach, erupting acid into her throat. It is sour and unwelcome.

Artimar does not understand. His stepson. Her mother. Lara takes the photos from Susan, who had the forethought to bring them to the shop, and hands them to Artimar.

"This is why she sent me to the shop," Lara mumbles to herself. "Virginia knew who raped her. She wanted me to know my father. What I don't get," Lara is talking to Susan now, "is how she found him. If she knew who raped her, why didn't she tell the police?"

Lara, chilled, is shaking. "I hate him, Artimar. I hate your stepson."

Only the fan is audible to her now. Susan's mouth is moving, and Lara can see that she is explaining things to Artimar, pointing at the photos. He looks from the pictures to Lara several times, an expression of disbelief on his face.

Reading about the rape in her mother's letter was hard, but seeing photos of Virginia standing there, vulnerable, hopeful, and unaware, blisters Lara's spirit. Photos of the gray cement where she was conceived bring back the gagging odor of her adoptive father's drunken breath. Virginia could not escape either. Lara gags on the familiarity of her mother's entrapment. How many times did she try to wash him away?

Artimar moves closer, his brow bent with concern, "I'm not his father, but I'd be honored to have you as a grandchild. There are no words…child."

Lara does not acknowledge his sorrow. Hers is too sharp.

"She's in shock." Lara hears Susan explaining her rude behavior.

Without uttering a word, Lara leaves the shop.

Chapter 45

June 18, 1991

Walking, lost in thought, Lara travels several blocks before realizing that she is back on Bay Street. A missing criminal and a dead woman accompany her, invisible, untouchable.

Thomas Pearce is her soothsayer. Yet, no matter how detailed his telling, crucial layers are missing. Filtered by his life experience, her birth family becomes cinematic. Some memories Thomas shares are vivid transporters to the past, but when the story ends, she is a mere spectator.

Lara crosses crowded sidewalks, walking on the cobbled street to reach the river. *If all I get are photos and stories, maybe not knowing would be better.* The thought is foreign and goes against everything Lara has believed. Knowing is the Holy Grail. Knowing is all she's ever wanted.

The river at her side, Lara continues the solemn march to the statue. The face is not her mother's, yet that is all she can see in the dark mood. Standing in front of Savannah's Waving Girl is as close as she will ever be to her birth mother. Lara aches to touch the face just once.

Susan finds her sitting at the statue's base, silent. There are no words shared as Susan gathers Lara's purse, hugs her shoulders hard, and takes her to the car.

"My place?" Susan asks, and from a veil of grief, Lara nods.

Lara's mood is a stark contrast to the animal prints and pink walls of Susan's living room. Lara dials her uncle's number. "Hello, Thomas. I'll be back in an hour or so. I found something you need to see. I know his name."

"Whose name?" Thomas asks.

"The photographer," Lara answers. "I'll show you when I get there. Just need some time to digest it, you know?"

Sitting with Susan clears her head enough to allow in a sliver of sunshine. "He cares, you know, Susan. I don't know how I can show him the photos. He's gonna be sick. It's his sister."

"Girl, you have to show him. Those photos might get that mother of yours some justice."

"Did you hear Artimar? He asked to be my grandfather. Was he okay when you left him?"

"He was upset, mostly because he let his stepson get away. He had no idea though. Just thought the birdbrain was irresponsible, never figured him to be violent."

Susan sips on something from a tiny demitasse cup. "What's that?" Lara asks.

"Jägermeister. It's German. Want some?"

"Yes, please."

Susan gets up to pour her a drink from the globe-shaped bar in the corner of her dining room.

"They're pretty generous, Artimar and my uncle both offering to act like relatives."

"Thomas is your kin, Lara."

Susan hands her a tiny teal glass and Lara smells it. "Licorice?"

"Better than any candy I ever ate. Cheers, to your new family."

"A toast to my getting used to new family." Lara downs the liquid.

Calmer, Lara says, "This place suits you, Susan. I like the cow." A menagerie of life-size toy animals surrounds them in the fuchsia and black living room, and a four-foot high cow wearing a pink feather boa dominates the room.

"Nevah lonely with them starin' at me," Susan says.

"May I use your phone again for a long distance call? I need to call my mom. I'll pay you for the call." Lara reaches for her purse.

"Pay, shmay. Just call your momma, girl." Susan takes the glasses to the kitchen, giving Lara privacy.

"Hi, Mom. What are you doing home?"

"Worrying sick about you."

The pang of guilt usually associated with such motherly comments fails to blossom. Instead, a bloom of thanks settles around the call. "I'm sorry I haven't called. A lot has happened."

"I called the hotel, and they said you were checked out. Where are you, Lara?"

"At a girlfriend's. Listen I have to tell you something important."

"I'm listening."

"I found my birth family. My birth mother is dead."

"Oh, Lara, I...What the hell am I supposed to say to that?"

"Mom. I'm okay. It's okay. I'm staying at my uncle's. I am coming home soon, okay?"

"Okay. I can't believe you did it, Lara. Is he nice?"

"Very. I will call you before I leave, okay?"

"Okay. I'm glad you're okay, and Lara..."

"Yes, Mom."

"I'm sorry...that she's dead. Sure you're okay?"

"It's okay, Mom. I'm fine. I love you, Mom. I'll call you tomorrow."

"I love you too, Lara."

Lara is about to hang up when her mother says, "Oh, almost forgot to tell you. Margaret got a job in Manhattan at an ad agency as president. Can you imagine, Lara? I hear she's getting three figures. Aunt Connie can't stop talking about it."

"Wow, that's great, Mom. Tell her I said congrats, okay? Gotta run. Bye."

"Susan," Lara yells. "You can stop hiding now."

Susan, who has been listening from the kitchen, says, "I'm not hiding. I'm eating devil dogs and overhearing."

The same cousin gossip that would have sent Lara into a tailspin of insecurity just a few weeks prior makes her smile. There is comfort in the cast of characters that she has called family for so long. Unlike the stories shared by her new uncle, her mother's words are a quilt of memories.

With frailties and physical appearances she can play in her mind's eye, the New York family knows her. Each member hurt or heralded her growing up. Her mother did not tell her about Margaret's accomplishment to calm her, yet it is soothing just the same.

She is a part of Savannah and its people, but the fabric of her life is up north. The mention of Margaret has brought her to a crossroad, a place where she gets to decide just how much of each family she will incorporate into her life.

"Susan, I get to choose my family. Crazy, huh?"

"Sure, you get to pick from the best of two worlds. The rest of us are stuck with what we got."

In Susan's colorful living room, Lara reviews her birth mother's choices. Without a clue what would come of it, Virginia chose to write the letter that gave Lara her family. The information is free to do with as she wants. Tuck it away, share it; the choice is hers. Unlike her mother, she will not become a victim of the rape and relinquishment. Unlike the nightmare years of her childhood with its planned escapes and lack of means to carry them out, this is in Lara's complete control.

She might not decide this minute, or tomorrow, or next year, but it doesn't matter because she owns it. There is no way to reverse what happened to Virginia. Equipped with the knowledge of where she comes from, Lara has no idea where she will go next, except to the police.

Chapter 46

June 19, 1991

The police station is surprisingly quiet, only a few people line the benches of the waiting area. Thomas agreed to meet her, and the hard bench seems a perfect place to show him the harsh photos.

"I'm sorry to show them to you here, but you need to see them. They're horrible."

Lara hands him the photos, and Thomas moves through them quickly. No need to wallow on the scene, it is perfectly clear that the photos are from the rape.

"She's still pushy," Thomas says.

"What do you mean?"

"That camera, and these," her uncle explains. "No way it's coincidence. Has to be her, still pushing buttons, even in heaven."

Lara likes to think of her birth mother watching over her, placing props in her path. *Did she know about the camera, or just the fact that the man who raped her lived over the shop?*

Together, Thomas and Lara approach the front desk, "We'd like to talk to someone about a crime from 1970," Thomas says.

"1970. Whoa, that's an oldie," the silver-haired receptionist replies.

"Yes, we know. We have some new evidence."

"Let me see if Randolph is in. He was chief back then. Retired for three years now, but we can't seem to get rid of him."

They sit in the waiting area again and Thomas taps the envelope of evidence on his knee.

"I remember when my sister was chosen to pose for that man. We were all so proud but those photos…she must have been devastated. At least she looks happy in the photos we can see her in."

Thomas takes the photos out again. "She looks so proud and beautiful." Thomas is going through the pile when a grizzled pip of a man interrupts. His uniform is threadbare at the knees and appears two sizes too large.

"How do? I'm Randolph. Hear you have an old case to frustrate me with," he says frowning.

"Well, sir, we hope to de-frustrate you, actually," Lara assures him.

"Come on back. Let's see what you have."

A half-eaten tuna sandwich sits at the corner of the retired chief's desk, and Lara believes she understands his initial frustration. "We interrupted your lunch? Perhaps we can come back later."

"Nah, I hate tuna, but no matter how many times I've told my wife that in the past thirty-seven years, she still packs it."

He tosses the sandwich into a black lunchbox and pushes aside papers to make room for his folded hands. "Tell me what you have."

"We're here about a rape case from 1970. Virginia Senton was the victim," Lara starts.

"Go on." Randolph taps his watch and lifts it to hear if it is ticking.

"Well, she was raped by someone claiming to be a photographer working for the sculptor of the Waving Girl statue," Lara says.

208

"I'll be damned, I remember that one. Can't recall much about it, 'cept I sweat bullets when I had to call the artist. De Well…something or other. He made that statue in Washington. You know, the Marines with the flag. He was pretty upset too. Artsy type, you know?"

The inference annoys Lara. De Weldon may have been artsy, but he honored her mother in a way the chief will never understand.

"Well, Virginia was my sister," Thomas says.

"And my mother," Lara adds.

"That case has been cold for twenty years. I'll have to requisition the file. Hang on, wasn't a murder was it?"

Thomas and Lara answer simultaneously, "No, she was raped."

"Good, then you're in luck. Couple years back the state removed the statute of limitations for prosecution of kidnapping and rape. So we can open her back up, depending on what you have."

"We have these." Thomas hands him the envelope of photos.

Randolph puts on his glasses to look at the photographs. "No perp, just the victim, right?"

"Yes, but I also have the camera the film came from," Lara says, "and I can tell you who it belonged to. His name is Harlan Dunbar, and he left this," she hands him the camera, "at his stepfather's home after the crime. He disappeared after that."

"Any idea where he is now?"

"No idea. His stepfather owns the Enchanted Violin, an antique shop downtown."

"Can't promise anything, but I'll take a look. Will the stepfather talk to me?"

"Yes, I think so," Lara answers.

"Leave your number with Flo at the front desk. She'll give you a call if we find anything."

Thomas and Lara leave the police department arm in arm. "My gift to you, Virginia," she says, looking up. "Even if they never find him, at least he's accountable, in name anyway, for what he did."

"I know," Thomas says. "We should celebrate. Ideas?"

Lara asks, "Where is she buried?"

"Not exactly what I had in mind. She's in the family plot at Laurel Grove Cemetery. My parents are also there."

"I'd like to pay my respects." Lara dreads seeing the stone with Virginia's name but knows it's important.

"She'd like that. I'll take you," Thomas offers.

Lara hesitates. "This might be something I need to do alone."

"I can stay in the car if you want. It's not in the greatest neighborhood."

"That works. Mind if we stop at a flower shop?"

"Not at all. There's a place on the way."

Abel is closing when they pull up. His big gold grin appears the minute he spots Lara.

"Well, Miss Lara, some pretty special kids have been getting your flowers. I delivered three arrangements to the children's ward at Memorial."

"He is persistent, huh?" Lara shakes her head. "If more orders come in, keep sending them there. Think you could stay open a minute more? I need flowers for my mother's grave."

Putting the key back in the lock and turning off the alarm, Abel locks the door behind them. "Anything for my best customer," he chuckles. "What would you like?"

Lara looks around the shop and spies a large arrangement of sunflowers in the cooler. "How about those?"

"On the house."

"People in Savannah keep giving me stuff." Lara smiles weakly. "It's a miracle you stay in business. Well, I guess this is goodbye again."

"Not goodbye. You'll be back. You'll be back," Abel says, waving at Thomas in the driver's seat and gesturing for her to get in. As they drive off, Lara watches Abel lock the shop and start his slow saunter to River Street.

Chapter 47

June 19, 1991

Standing in front of her mother's grave makes the world small. Her feet are heavy, cemented to the finding spot. All Lara has searched for is on the stone. Virginia Senton's dates and labels appear there: daughter, sister. One is missing—mother.

The information is there but the person she has ached to know for so long is lost. The days since she found the letter in the Bible have been spent in pursuit of life. Looking at the stone and those around it, she understands that no matter how ornate or detailed, the stone cannot capture the life buried beneath it.

Her mother's suffering is not there. Her brave transfer of information to a child she could not keep is not there. The car accident is not there. Lara touches the smooth granite face, tracing the letters of Virginia's name with her finger.

Kneeling before the grave, she brushes branches away and speaks quietly, "Well, Mom, I got your letter. I'm here. I found you."

Tears fill Lara's eyes. "I know what you went through, and I'm sorry you had such sadness. I also found the antique shop. I know who he is too. Thomas and I gave his name to the police."

Tears wash her cheeks now. "I wish I'd known you. I really do. I wish you'd known me too. I think we would have liked each other. I look just like you."

She stops, her throat constricted from emotion. "I know you probably thought about me a lot and if I was angry. I'm not. You did what you had to, and no matter what, I'll always love you."

Unsure what else to say, Lara prays the Lord's Prayer silently. A tear falls on her mother's grave as she moves the flowers to the front of the stone. Walking away, Lara feels the weight of wondering disappear. Part of her wants to turn back one more time, but Lara knows that Virginia would not want her to spend her precious time in Savannah at a grave.

Lara pictures Virginia standing in the shaded spot, watching her depart, waving, and smiling because all has been revealed to her only child. Without turning, Lara lifts her right hand to her left shoulder and waves right back.

Thomas is standing outside the car and asks as she approaches, "I'd like to pay my respects. Mind waiting?"

"Of course not." Lara watches him walk towards his sister's grave. *He's my blood. A good man. I'll keep in touch with him.* Gazing up at the canopy of majestic oaks and recalling her first time in the cemetery she realizes, *Full circle, I'm done.*

On the drive back to Thomas's house, Lara contemplates Robert's dishonor for the first time in days. The recent flurry of discoveries and emotions made it easy not to explore that hurt. Lara believed he was honest and that she would fill the place in Robert's heart left empty by his parents. A part of her still wants to believe that he loved her.

Lara wishes she could tell Robert about her new family. She wants him to know that connections are not always living, but they can be built from memories, photographs, and stories. She wants to tell him that sometimes people must reach beyond the connections they dream of and embrace the ones they are given.

"Lara, I have a date tonight." Thomas looks down bashfully. "I had it scheduled before you...arrived. I'll cancel if you like."

"No way. I'll call Susan. Go on your date."

"Hey, gal. How's my favorite Savannah snoop today?" Susan is chipper as always.

"Thomas and I went to the police today, and I just visited Virginia's grave. I feel like someone ran me through a wash cycle, but otherwise I'm pretty calm. I think I am ready to go home."

"What? And leave me to the doldrums of decorating? When do you leave?"

"Tomorrow, I think."

"Well, girlfriend, let's whoop up a goodbye shindig. How about Mercury's?"

"Sounds like a plan. I'll tell my uncle to meet us there. He has a date. What time?"

"He's single after all. I knew it. Hiding him from me? Nine o'clock. Wear something flashy. Might as well leave 'em talking."

Lara laughs. "Since when have I not worn something flashy?"

Chapter 48

June 19, 1991

Upstairs is busy. Lara wishes they could sit downstairs which looks much emptier. Only a few college kids line the bar.

Susan says, "No way. I like 'em legal age." She spots two empty stools upstairs, ordering them cosmos. "To new friends and family." Susan lifts her glass.

"To keeping in touch," Lara adds before touching the extra-large glass to Susan's.

"So, what will you do with the rest of your summer?"

"Not sure. Not much of the student loan money left. I'll have to get a job."

"Why not stay then. You could work with me for the rest of the summer. You're certainly welcome to crash at my place."

Tempting, Lara muses. She has not really considered staying in Savannah. "I don't know, Susan. I just feel ready to go home. Can't explain it. Guess I feel like this chapter's closed. I'm ready to go back to read the introduction again. Might be nice not having anything to search for any more. I just have to figure out how to fit it all together."

"I think I get it. You need your old stomping ground. Missing home?"

"Yeah, that is part of it. Just need to be where nothing is new or different, except, of course, me."

Susan orders a second drink, and Lara can't fathom where this itsy bitsy woman is putting all the alcohol. Her mom used to call it a wooden leg.

"Sad." Susan is watching a drunk woman spin alone on the dance floor, stumbling.

"It is," Lara says. "Does anyone ever talk to her like a real person?"

"Never seen it. Dolly's been coming here for years."

"Where does she live?" Lara watches as the woman tugs at torn pantyhose that are a shade too dark.

"Not sure. I think she stays at the Pine Street shelter. Saw her sitting out front once in the afternoon. Waiting for the party to begin, I guess." Dolly continues to bounce and wiggle her way around the room until she bumps into a man, toppling his drink. Perturbed, he turns to see who wasted his nine-dollar martini.

"It's Robert." Lara looks at Susan.

"Uh oh," is all Susan can muster.

Robert spots them immediately and moves without hesitation to put his glass on one of the counters that protrude from the black walls. He does not take his eyes off Lara and moves with a swiftness that leaves her no time to plan what she will say.

"Lara." His tone is cold and questioning.

"Hello, Robert. How are you?"

"How am I? I thought you left Savannah. Why didn't you meet me after the tour? I sent flowers. Did you get them?"

"I got them, Robert." She is eyeing the wet stain on his pressed white shirt. "I just figured your new friend might enjoy them more than me."

"What new friend?"

"Let's not play games, Robert. I saw you with her after the first tour. I was at the lion fountain. The truth is the truth. So let's drop it, okay?"

"Are you talking about Karen?

"Uh, I'm not privy to her name, only to the fact that she seems quite beholden to you. She must have loved the medallion you found for her."

"I did not find a medallion for her."

"Oh, excuse me. I meant to say crafted. You are quite the artist."

Susan stirs her cosmo nervously as the conversation grows more heated.

"Lara, listen. Can we talk for a minute, outside?"

The band is playing and he is having trouble hearing her.

"Sure, I have nothing to hide." She smiles at Susan and places her purse on the stool to save her spot.

Moving through the crowded room and down the stairs, Robert puts his arm on Lara's shoulder. She shrugs it off, glaring. Who is he kidding? Lara has not realized until this moment just how angry she is at him. *How dare he take advantage of me?*

Outside, the street is surprisingly tranquil. Down the street at city market, an outdoor trio plays acoustic music and the sound tiptoes through the street, arriving on a breeze and leaving just as quickly.

From Mercury, they turn left, heading towards the parking garage. Robert is silent. Lara wants to scream but decides that hollering at this time of night might gain unwanted attention. They stop at a bench at the corner of Congress and Barnard Streets. Lara looks into the eyes she found so compelling. Weariness and anger replaces the mystery. For a moment, she worries about her safety, but reasons that while he's woefully misguided and in need of some decent therapy, Robert is not a physical danger.

He stares at her for a full, awkward minute. "Lara, I miss you."

"Tell," she pauses, trying to recall the name. "Oh yeah, tell Karen all about it, Robert. I may be new around here, but I'm not a fool."

"Karen is my replacement, Lara."

"Don't you mean my replacement?"

"I quit the trolley. I knew you were leery about the job, the women, and it didn't feel right anymore. So I resigned. The woman you saw me with was Karen Kincaid, a new guide. I was training her."

"Training her on the medallions? I saw you take her there."

"Actually, I was showing her around the historic district, and she asked about my family. Her parents are members of the historical society in Charleston. I showed her the lobby and gave her a tour of the bank." Robert runs a hand through his hair, clearly frustrated.

Lara is quiet. It makes sense that he'd train a replacement, but she finds it hard to swallow such a speedy hire. "When did you quit?"

"The day before you saw me with Karen. I was going to tell you at dinner. I know you've been jealous of the other women. The job is not worth losing your trust." Robert is pacing now. "When you didn't return my calls and the hotel said you checked out, I figured you left Savannah. Why didn't you call me on what you saw?"

Lara considers the possibility of his innocence and whether her detective skills might be that off kilter.

"When I saw you take her into the bank, I thought— Tell me this, why did she hug you? I saw her hug you. Looked cozy."

"She was thanking me for showing her around, that's all. I'm not going to defend what I did before, but for God's sake Lara, you have to believe me."

Lara can't decide if he is sincere and has a gnawing feeling that she should have at least let him explain.

"Robert." She does not know what to say. Rather than address his anger or her failed assumptions, Lara retreats behind the revelation of what has happened since they parted.

"I found my mother, Robert. She's dead, killed in a car crash. She was a member of Altrusa Club like we thought."

Robert stops pacing but does not interrupt, so she continues. "There were two more letters hidden in a key box at Pearce's house. He IS my uncle. It has been...so much has happened. I'm sorry. I should have asked about the woman that I saw you with. It was just, well, it seemed so obvious."

"I was honest, Lara. I thought you believed me."

"I tried," she whispers, looking towards the club.

"Tried? So you don't believe me?" Robert is standing in front of her now, close enough to recall the smell of him and wish for a needy, freshly pressed kiss like the first one they shared.

"So much has changed Robert," she says, and he reaches out to her.

"Not this." His hands touch her face and, stroking her cheeks gently with his thumbs, he draws her forward, covering her lips with a kiss. Lara kisses him back, knowing it is goodbye, and savoring what is fast becoming a memory instead of an ache.

"Lara." He backs away to speak. "Why didn't you ask me about what you saw?"

"I didn't trust you all the way, Robert. I tried, but with the stuff Abel told me, and what you admitted about the women and the medallions...you seem sort of, well, lost. We had that in common."

He looks confused until realization lifts his brows. Robert says, "Not had, we *are* connected, Lara. The Pearce medallion is real. Your truth was in that lobby all along. It's more than coincidence that you took my tour."

"Not coincidence, no. I'm so glad we met. Without you, I might not have found...all of it, my story. You helped me find it, and I'll never forget it."

"Jesus, Lara that sounds a hell of a lot like goodbye."

Robert sits on the bench now and with head in hands says, "You have to give us a chance. I've been worried sick. I sent flowers even after they said you checked out, hoping that

Bloom guy might know where you were. I should have asked him." Robert rubs his forehead in frustration, "Crap, this is crap, Lara."

Lara sits beside him, touching his shoulder, and says, "Abel didn't know where I was Robert. I'm staying at my uncle's house in my birth mother's old room."

"Amazing," Robert says without enthusiasm. "Let's just forget about all of this. Clean the slate, okay? We can have lunch tomorrow, talk it all out."

Lara kisses his cheek, hoping to prepare him for the hurt. "Robert, my search is over. I'm leaving. I found what I was looking for in Savannah, but you haven't."

"What is that supposed to mean?"

"When we met, I was searching for my…foundation. We both were. I needed to know my history, and you needed to make peace with yours. You still do."

Robert nods. "This is your foundation, Lara." He opens his arms and stands to indicate the city. "Savannah is OUR foundation."

"Yes, but I have a foundation at home, too, and a family that needs me."

"You'll be back." Robert says, his ego resurfacing. "You can leave Savannah, but it will never leave you."

Lara touches Robert's hand to her heart. "I know, Robert. Savannah is here, forever."

Chapter 49

June 20, 1991

Packing her suitcase and laying it on her birth mother's bed, Lara lingers in the room, touching as many of the precious personal items from her life as possible. As she holds the mirror that once revealed a reflection so like hers, a spirit of relief and longing intermingles with the sorrow of having to leave.

The closet is last. No longer the fragmented child hiding to escape, Lara opens the door, hoping once again to discover the essence of her birth mother. Standing where Virginia stood to choose an outfit for the dreaded trip to New York, Lara imagines the soft skin of her mother's arm brushing hers as she reaches for a garment. *Were her clothes tight? Was she showing?* Lara presses each garment to her lips, whispering goodbye to the ghostly presence of her life-giver.

Her uncle stands at the bottom of the staircase when she emerges carrying her case. He smiles sweetly and rushes to help her with the bag. A neatly wrapped package sits on the entry table. Her uncle puts down her suitcase on the Oriental rug and hands her the gift.

"Open it at home. Okay?"

"Sure," she whispers. Overwhelmed with emotion, she grabs his shoulders for a hug.

Hugging her back, he whispers, "Goodbye, Lara. Please remember this is your place. You are welcome anytime. You're family, and so is your other mom. She raised a beautiful woman. Thank her for me."

"Thank you, thank you for all of this. I don't know what to say."

Awkward yet caring, they hug more tightly as neither can find the right words.

As she pulls away from the curb, her uncle stands at the top of the front steps. His waving silhouette shrinks in her rearview mirror as she drives away. Lara is weepy with goodbyes. She thought the hardest part of leaving Savannah would be giving up Robert, but it is splitting from what she found that weighs heaviest on her heart.

Waving over her shoulder at the blurred, far-away reflection of the man she now calls uncle, she turns the corner, passing the last lush square she will see in Savannah. She is heading north. Unhurried, she counts the church steeples and memorizes the bend of each oak tree before getting back on Interstate 16. Lara starts missing Savannah before it is five miles behind her.

The trip seems shorter than the one to Savannah, and Lara is soon driving through the honking traffic of New York City towards home. Pulling up to the three-story house, she feels oddly relieved. The cracked sidewalk that leads to the door and every mismatched carpeted step are part of her. Dragging her suitcase and carrying her uncle's gift, she climbs the steps.

Her mother is sitting at the kitchen table, stirring a cup of coffee and reading the newspaper. Her face lights up the minute she sees Lara. Maureen stands, "Well, it's about time." The words are expectant, fearful, relieved.

"Hi, Mom."

Lara waits for the onslaught of questions and chastisements. Instead, Maureen moves closer to her to hug her stiffly. For the first time, Lara experiences her mother's hug as belonging. *This is family,* she decides, holding her mother closer and feeling her mother respond. *This is found.*

"What's that?" Maureen asks about the gift, ending the embrace.

"Not sure. My uncle said to open it at home."

"Well, open it then." Maureen is at the sink, washing her mug.

Lara does as she is told.

Inside the gift box is the photo of Virginia from her uncle's music room. The same one her uncle took from the piano to show her at their first meeting.

"Mom, come here."

Maureen looks at the expensive framed photo and the smiling woman in the picture who looks so much like her daughter.

Putting a supportive arm around her mother's waist Lara says, "Mom, meet my mother. This is Virginia."

About the Author

V.L. Brunskill has been a professional writer for twenty years. She ditched journalism class after landing her very first interview with the late, great, punk icon Joey Ramone. As a national music journalist, V.L. has written for publications such as *Metronome* magazine, *CREEM*, *The Boston Globe*, and *Boston Phoenix*. From hundreds of rock star interviews to rocking ions, V.L. went on to become a technical writer in the semiconductor and IT fields.

Born in Brooklyn, New York, on Christmas Eve, and adopted after seven months, V.L. was reborn in 1991, when she was reunited with her biological parents. She moved south to be closer to both. V.L. assists other adoptees to search on her blog adoptionfind.wordpress.com

V.L. lives in Savannah, Georgia, with her bass-player husband, above-average daughter, and delightfully bad dog.

"Searching is difficult. Finding is life-altering."
-V.L. Brunskill

CPSIA information can be obtained at www.ICGtesting.com
Printed in the USA
BVOW03s2218120715

408380BV00001B/62/P